"I ain't fergot dat ar 'possum."

JOEL CHANDLER HARRIS

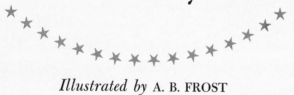

The Chronicles
of
Aunt Minervy Ann

Illustrated by A. B. FROST

The American Short Story Series

VOLUME 21

GARRETT PRESS

Library of Congress Catalog Card No. 68-55680

*This volume was reprinted from the 1899 edition
published by Charles Scribner's Sons*
First Garrett Press Edition published 1969

The American Short Story Series
Volume 21
© 1968

Manufactured in the United States of America

GARRETT PRESS, INC.
Publishers
250 West 54th Street, New York, N.Y. 10019

CONTENTS

LIST OF ILLUSTRATIONS

LIST OF ILLUSTRATIONS

viii

LIST OF ILLUSTRATIONS

THE CHRONICLES OF
AUNT MINERVY ANN

I

AN EVENING WITH THE KU-KLUX

THE happiest, the most vivid, and certainly the most critical period of a man's life is combined in the years that stretch between sixteen and twenty-two. His responsibilities do not sit heavily on him, he has hardly begun to realize them, and yet he has begun to see and feel, to observe and absorb; he is for once and for the last time an interested, and yet an irresponsible, spectator of the passing show.

This period I had passed very pleasantly, if not profitably, at Halcyondale in Middle Georgia, directly after the great war, and the town and the people there had a place apart, in my mind. When, therefore, some ten years after leaving there, I received a cordial invitation to attend the county fair, which had been organized by some of the enterprising spirits of the town and county, among whom

1

were Paul Conant and his father-in-law, Major Tumlin Perdue, it was natural that the fact should revive old memories.

The most persistent of these memories were those which clustered around Major Perdue, his daughter Vallie, and his brother-in-law, Colonel Bolivar Blasengame, and Aunt Minervy Ann Perdue. Curiously enough, my recollection of this negro woman was the most persistent of all. Her individuality seemed to stand out more vitally than the rest. She was what is called " a character," and something more besides. The truth is, I should have missed a good deal if I had never known Aunt Minervy Ann Perdue, who, as she described herself, was " Affikin fum 'way back yander 'fo' de flood, an' fum de word go "—a fact which seriously interferes with the somewhat complacent theory that Ham, son of Noah, was the original negro.

It is a fact that Aunt Minervy Ann's great-grandmother, who lived to be a hundred and twenty years old, had an eagle tattooed on her breast, the mark of royalty. The brother of this princess, Qua, who died in Augusta at the age of one hundred years, had two eagles tattooed on his breast. This, taken in connection with his name, which means The Eagle, shows that he was either the ruler of his tribe or

2

the heir apparent. The prince and princess were very small, compared with the average African, but the records kept by a member of the Clopton family show that during the Revolution Qua performed some wonderful feats, and went through some strange adventures in behalf of liberty. He was in his element when war was at its hottest—and it has never been hotter in any age or time, or in any part of the world, savage or civilized, than it was then in the section of Georgia now comprised in the counties of Burke, Columbia, Richmond, and Elbert.

However, that has nothing to do with Aunt Minervy Ann Perdue; but her relationship to Qua and to the royal family of his tribe, remote though it was, accounted for the most prominent traits of her character, and many contradictory elements of her strong and sharply defined individuality. She had a bad temper, and was both fierce and fearless when it was aroused; but it was accompanied by a heart as tender and a devotion as unselfish as any mortal ever possessed or displayed. Her temper was more widely advertised than her tenderness, and her independence more clearly in evidence than her unselfish devotion, except to those who knew her well or intimately.

3

And so it happened that Aunt Minervy Ann, after freedom gave her the privilege of showing her extraordinary qualities of self-sacrifice, walked about in the midst of the suspicion and distrust of her own race, and was followed by the misapprehensions and misconceptions of many of the whites. She knew the situation and laughed at it, and if she wasn't proud of it her attitude belied her.

It was at the moment of transition from the old conditions to the new that I had known Aunt Minervy Ann and the persons in whom she was so profoundly interested, and she and they, as I have said, had a place apart in my memory and experience. I also remembered Hamp, Aunt Minervy Ann's husband, and the queer contrast between the two. It was mainly on account of Hamp, perhaps, that Aunt Minervy Ann was led to take such a friendly interest in the somewhat lonely youth who was editor, compositor, and pressman of Halcyondale's ambitious weekly newspaper in the days following the collapse of the confederacy.

When a slave, Hamp had belonged to an estate which was in the hands of the Court of Ordinary (or, as it was then called, the Inferior Court), to be administered in the interest of minor heirs. This was not a fortunate thing for the negroes, of which

4

there were above one hundred and fifty. Men, women, and children were hired out, some far and some near. They came back home at Christmastime, enjoyed a week's frolic, and were then hired out again, perhaps to new employers. But whether to new or old, it is certain that hired hands in those days did not receive the consideration that men gave to their own negroes.

This experience told heavily on Hamp's mind. It made him reserved, suspicious, and antagonistic. He had few pleasant memories to fall back on, and these were of the days of his early youth, when he used to trot around holding to his old master's coattails—the kind old master who had finally been sent to the insane asylum. Hamp never got over the idea (he had heard some of the older negroes talking about it) that his old master had been judged to be crazy simply because he was unusually kind to his negroes, especially the little ones. Hamp's afterexperience seemed to prove this, for he received small share of kindness, as well as scrimped rations, from the majority of those who hired him.

It was a very good thing for Hamp that he married Aunt Minervy Ann, otherwise he would have become a wanderer and a vagabond when freedom came. It was a fate he didn't miss a hair's breadth;

5

he " broke loose," as he described it, and went off, but finally came back and tried in vain to persuade Aunt Minervy Ann to leave Major Perdue. He finally settled down, but acquired no very friendly feelings toward the white race.

He joined the secret political societies, strangely called " Union Leagues," and aided in disseminating the belief that the whites were only awaiting a favorable opportunity to re-enslave his race. He was only repeating what the carpet-baggers had told him. Perhaps he believed the statement, perhaps not. At any rate, he repeated it fervently and frequently, and soon came to be the recognized leader of the negroes in the county of which Halcyondale was the capital. That is to say, the leader of all except one. At church one Sunday night some of the brethren congratulated Aunt Minervy Ann on the fact that Hamp was now the leader of the colored people in that region.

" What colored people? " snapped Aunt Minervy Ann.

" We-all," responded a deacon, emphatically.

" Well, he can't lead *me*, I'll tell you dat right now! " exclaimed Aunt Minervy Ann.

Anyhow, when the time came to elect members of the Legislature (the constitutional convention

"Well, he can't lead *me*."

had already been held), Hamp was chosen to be the candidate of the negro Republicans. A white man wanted to run, but the negroes said they preferred their own color, and they had their way. They had their way at the polls, too, for, as nearly all the whites who would have voted had served in the Confederate army, they were at that time disfranchised.

So Hamp was elected overwhelmingly, "worl' widout een'," as he put it, and the effect it had on him was a perfect illustration of one aspect of human nature. Before and during the election (which lasted three days) Hamp had been going around puffed up with importance. He wore a blue army overcoat and a stove-pipe hat, and went about smoking a big cigar. When the election was over, and he was declared the choice of the county, he collapsed. His dignity all disappeared. His air of self-importance and confidence deserted him. His responsibilities seemed to weigh him down.

He had once "rolled" in the little printing-office where the machinery consisted of a No. 2 Washington hand-press, a wooden imposing-stone, three stands for the cases, a rickety table for "wetting down" the paper, and a tub in which to wash the forms. This office chanced to be my headquarters,

7

and the day after the election I was somewhat surprised to see Hamp saunter in. So was Major Tumlin Perdue, who was reading the exchanges.

" He's come to demand a retraction," remarked the Major, " and you'll have to set him right. He's no longer plain Hamp; he's the Hon. Hamp— what's your other name? " turning to the negro.

" Hamp Tumlin my fergiven name, suh. I thought 'Nervy Ann tol' you dat."

" Why, who named you after me? " inquired the Major, somewhat angrily.

" Me an' 'Nervy Ann fix it up, suh. She say it's about de purtiest name in town."

The Major melted a little, but his bristles rose again, as it were.

" Look here, Hamp! " he exclaimed in a tone that nobody ever forgot or misinterpreted; " don't you go and stick Perdue onto it. I won't stand that! "

" No, suh! " responded Hamp. " I started ter do it, but 'Nervy Ann say she ain't gwine ter have de Perdue name bandied about up dar whar de Legislatur's at."

Again the Major thawed, and though he looked long at Hamp it was with friendly eyes. He seemed to be studying the negro—" sizing him up," as the

8

He wore a blue army overcoat and a stove-pipe hat.

saying is. For a newly elected member of the Legislature, Hamp seemed to take a great deal of interest in the old duties he once performed about the office. He went first to the box in which the " roller " was kept, and felt of its surface carefully.

" You'll hatter have a bran new roller 'fo' de mont's out," he said, " an' I won't be here to he'p you make it."

Then he went to the roller-frame, turned the handle, and looked at the wooden cylinders. " Dey don't look atter it like I use ter, suh; an' dish yer frame monst'us shackly."

From there he passed to the forms where the advertisements remained standing. He passed his thumb over the type and looked at it critically. " Dey er mighty skeer'd dey'll git all de ink off," was his comment. Do what he would, Hamp couldn't hide his embarrassment.

Meanwhile, Major Perdue scratched off a few lines in pencil. " I wish you'd get this in Tuesday's paper," he said. Then he read: " The Hon. Hampton Tumlin, recently elected a member of the Legislature, paid us a pop-call last Saturday. We are always pleased to meet our distinguished fellow-townsman and representative. We trust Hon. Hampton Tumlin will call again when the Ku-Klux are in."

" Why, certainly," said I, humoring the joke.

" Sholy you-all ain't gwine put dat in de paper, is you? " inquired Hamp, in amazement.

" Of course," replied the Major; " why not? "

" Kaze, ef you does, I'm a ruint nigger. Ef 'Nervy Ann hear talk 'bout my name an' entitlements bein' in de paper, she'll quit me sho. Uh-uh! I'm gwine 'way fum here! " With that Hamp bowed and disappeared. The Major chuckled over his little joke, but soon returned to his newspaper. For a quarter of an hour there was absolute quiet in the room, and, as it seemed, in the entire building, which was a brick structure of two stories, the stairway being in the centre. The hallway was, perhaps, seventy-five feet long, and on each side, at regular intervals, there were four rooms, making eight in all, and, with one exception, variously occupied as lawyers' offices or sleeping apartments, the exception being the printing-office in which Major Perdue and I were sitting. This was at the extreme rear of the hallway.

I had frequently been struck by the acoustic properties of this hallway. A conversation carried on in ordinary tones in the printing-office could hardly be heard in the adjoining room. Transferred to the front rooms, however, or even to the sidewalk fac-

10

"Sholy you-all ain't gwine put dat in de paper, is you?"

ing the entrance to the stairway, the lightest tone was magnified in volume. A German professor of music, who for a time occupied the apartment opposite the printing-office, was so harassed by the thunderous sounds of laughter and conversation rolling back upon him that he tried to remedy the matter by nailing two thicknesses of bagging along the floor from the stairway to the rear window. This was, indeed, something of a help, but when the German left, being of an economical turn of mind, he took his bagging away with him, and once more the hallway was torn and rent, as you may say, with the lightest whisper.

Thus it happened that, while the Major and I were sitting enjoying an extraordinary season of calm, suddenly there came a thundering sound from the stairway. A troop of horse could hardly have made a greater uproar, and yet I knew that fewer than half a dozen people were ascending the steps. Some one stumbled and caught himself, and the multiplied and magnified reverberations were as loud as if the roof had caved in, carrying the better part of the structure with it. Some one laughed at the misstep, and the sound came to our ears with the deafening effect of an explosion. he party filed with a dull roar into one of the front rooms, the office of a harum-scarum young lawyer who had more empty bottles behind his door than he had ever had briefs on his desk.

"Well, the great Gemini!" exclaimed Major Perdue, "how do you manage to stand that sort of thing?"

I shrugged my shoulders and laughed, and was about to begin anew a very old tirade against caves and halls of thunder, when the Major raised a warning hand. Some one was saying——

"He hangs out right on ol' Major Perdue's lot. He's got a wife there."

"By jing!" exclaimed another voice; "is that so? Well, I don't wanter git mixed up wi' the Major. He may be wobbly on his legs, but I don't wanter be the one to run up ag'in 'im."

The Major pursed up his lips and looked at the ceiling, his attitude being one of rapt attention.

"Shucks!" cried another; "by the time the ol' cock gits his bellyful of dram, thunder wouldn't roust 'im."

A shrewd, foxy, almost sinister expression came over the Major's rosy face as he glanced at me. His left hand went to his goatee, an invariable signal of deep feeling, such as anger, grief, or serious trouble. Another voice broke in here, a voice that we both knew to be that of Larry Pulliam, a big Kentuckian who had refugeed to Halcyondale during the war.

"Blast it all!" exclaimed Larry Pulliam, "I hope the Major will come out. Me an' him hain't never butted heads yit, an' it's gittin' high time. Ef he comes out, you fellers jest go ahead with your rat-killin'. *I*'ll 'ten' to him."

"Why, you'd make two of him, Pulliam," said the young lawyer.

"Oh, I'll not hurt 'im; that is, not *much*—jest enough to let 'im know I'm livin' in the same village," replied Mr. Pulliam. The voice of the town bull could not have had a more terrifying sound.

Glancing at the Major, I saw that he had entirely recovered his equanimity. More than that, a smile of sweet satisfaction and contentment settled on his rosy face, and stayed there.

"I wouldn't take a hundred dollars for that last remark," whispered the Major. "That chap's been a-raisin' his hackle at me ever since he's been here, and every time I try to get him to make a flutter he's off and gone. Of course it wouldn't do for me to push a row on him just dry so. But now——" The Major laughed softly, rubbed his hands together, and seemed to be as happy as a child with a new toy.

"My son," said he after awhile, "ain't there

13

some way of finding out who the other fellows are? Ain't you got some word you want Seab Griffin "— this was the young lawyer—" to spell for you? "

Spelling was the Major's weakness. He was a well-educated man, and could write vigorous English, but only a few days before he had asked me how many *f*'s there are in *graphic*.

" Let's see," he went on, rubbing the top of his head. " Do you spell *Byzantium* with two *y*'s, or with two *i*'s, or with one *y* and one *i*? It'll make Seab feel right good to be asked that before company, and he certainly needs to feel good if he's going with that crowd."

So, with a manuscript copy in my hand, I went hurriedly down the hall and put the important question. Mr. Griffin was all politeness, but not quite sure of the facts in the case. But he searched in his books of reference, including the Geographical Gazette, until finally he was able to give me the information I was supposed to stand in need of.

While he was searching, Mr. Pulliam turned to me and inquired what day the paper came out. When told that the date was Tuesday, he smiled and nodded his head mysteriously.

" That's good," he declared; " you'll be in time to ketch the news."

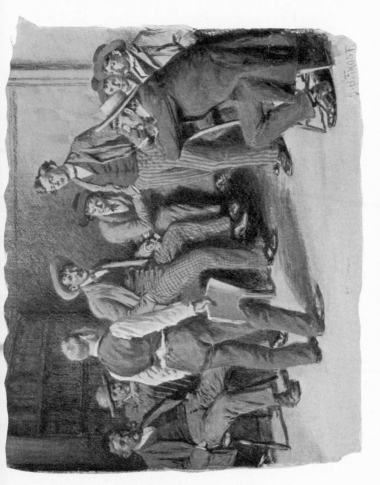

Inquired what day the paper came out.

" What news? " I inquired.

" Well, ef you don't hear about it before to-mor-rer night, jest inquire of Major Perdue. He'll tell you all about it."

Mr. Pulliam's tone was so supercilious that I was afraid the Major would lose his temper and come raging down the hallway. But he did nothing of the kind. When I returned he was fairly beaming, and seemed to be perfectly happy. The Major took down the names in his note-book—I have forgotten all except those of Buck Sanford and Larry Pulliam; they were all from the country except Larry Pulliam and the young lawyer.

After my visit to the room, the men spoke in lower tones, but every word came back to us as distinctly as before.

" The feed of the horses won't cost us a cent," remarked young Sanford. " Tom Gresham said he'd 'ten' to that. They're in the stable right now. And we're to have supper in Tom's back room, have a little game of ante, and along about twelve or one we'll sa'nter down and yank that darned nigger from betwixt his blankets, ef he's got any, and leave him to cool off at the cross-roads. Won't you go 'long, Seab, and see it well done? "

" I'll go and see if the supper's well done, and I'll

take a shy at your ante," replied Mr. Griffin. " But when it comes to the balance of the programme— well, I'm a lawyer, you know, and you couldn't expect me to witness the affair. I might have to take your cases and prove an alibi, you know, and I couldn't conscientiously do that if I was on hand at the time."

" The Ku-Klux don't have to have alibis," suggested Larry Pulliam.

" Perhaps not, still—" Apparently Mr. Griffin disposed of the matter with a gesture.

When all the details of their plan had been carefully arranged, the amateur Ku-Klux went filing out, the noise they made dying away like the echoes of a storm.

Major Perdue leaned his head against the back of his chair, closed his eyes, and sat there so quietly that I thought he was asleep. But this was a mistake. Suddenly he began to laugh, and he laughed until the tears ran down his face. It was laughter that was contagious, and presently I found myself joining in without knowing why. This started the Major afresh, and we both laughed until exhaustion came to our aid.

" O Lord! " cried the Major, panting, " I haven't had as much fun since the war, and a long time before. That blamed Pulliam is going to walk into a trap of his own setting. Now you jest watch how he goes out ag'in."

"But I'll not be there," I suggested.

"Oh, yes!" exclaimed the Major, "you can't afford to miss it. It'll be the finest piece of news your paper ever had. You'll go to supper with me—" He paused. "No, I'll go home, send Valentine to her Aunt Emmy's, get Blasengame to come around, and we'll have supper about nine. That'll fix it. Some of them chaps might have an eye on my house, and I don't want 'em to see anybody but me go in there. Now, if you don't come at nine, I'll send Blasengame after you."

"I shall be glad to come, Major. I was simply fishing for an invitation."

"*That* fish is always on your hook, and you know it," the Major insisted.

As it was arranged, so it fell out. At nine, I lifted and dropped the knocker on the Major's front door. It opened so promptly that I was somewhat taken by surprise, but in a moment the hand of my host was on my arm, and he pulled me inside unceremoniously.

"I was on the lookout," the Major explained. "Minervy Ann has fixed to have waffles, and she's

crazy about havin' 'em just right. If she waits too
long to make 'em, the batter'll spoil; and if she puts
'em on before everybody's ready, they won't be
good. That's what she says. Here he is, you old
Hessian!" the Major cried, as Minervy Ann peeped
in from the dining-room. "Now slap that supper
together and let's get at it."

"I'r mighty glad you come, suh," said Aunt
Minervy Ann, with a courtesy and a smile, and then
she disappeared. In an incredibly short time supper was announced, and though Aunt Minervy has
since informed me confidentially that the Perdues
were having a hard time of it at that period, I'll do
her the justice to say that the supper she furnished
forth was as good as any to be had in that town—
waffles, beat biscuit, fried chicken, buttermilk, and
coffee that could not be surpassed.

"How about the biscuit, Minervy Ann?" inquired Colonel Blasengame, who was the Major's
brother-in-law, and therefore one of the family.

"I turned de dough on de block twelve times, an'
hit it a hundred an forty-sev'm licks," replied Aunt
Minervy Ann.

"I'm afeard you hit it one lick too many," said
Colonel Blasengame, winking at me.

"Well, suh, I been hittin' dat away a mighty

"I was on the lookout," the Major explained.

long time," Aunt Minervy Ann explained, " and I
ain't never hear no complaints."

" Oh, I'm not complainin', Minervy Ann." Colonel Blasengame waved his hand. " I'm mighty
glad you did hit the dough a lick too many. If you
hadn't, the biscuit would 'a' melted in my mouth,
and I believe I'd rather chew on 'em to get the
taste."

" He des runnin' on, suh," said Aunt Minervy
Ann to me. " Marse Bolivar know mighty well
dat he got ter go 'way fum de Nunited State fer ter
git any better biscuits dan what I kin bake."

Then there was a long pause, which was broken
by an attempt on the part of Major Perdue to give
Aunt Minervy Ann an inkling of the events likely
to happen during the night. She seemed to be both
hard of hearing and dull of understanding when
the subject was broached; or she may have suspected
the Major was joking or trying to " run a rig " on
her. Her questions and comments, however, were
very characteristic.

" I dunner what dey want wid Hamp," she said.
" Ef dey know'd how no-count he is, dey'd let 'im
'lone. What dey want wid 'im? "

" Well, two or three of the country boys and maybe some of the town chaps are going to call on him

19

between midnight and day. They want to take him out to the cross-roads. Hadn't you better fix 'em up a little snack? Hamp won't want anything, but the boys will feel a little hungry after the job is over."

"Nobody ain't never tell me dat de Legislatur' wuz like de Free Masons, whar dey have ter ride a billy goat an' go down in a dry well wid de chains a-clankin'. I done tol' Hamp dat he better not fool wid white folks' doin's."

"Only the colored members have to be initiated," explained the Major, solemnly.

"What does dey do wid um?" inquired Aunt Minervy Ann.

"Well," replied the Major, "they take 'em out to the nearest cross-roads, put ropes around their necks, run the ropes over limbs, and pull away as if they were drawing water from a well."

"What dey do dat fer?" asked Aunt Minervy Ann, apparently still oblivious to the meaning of it all.

"They want to see which'll break first, the ropes or the necks," the Major explained.

"Ef dey takes Hamp out," remarked Aunt Minervy Ann, tentatively—feeling her way, as it were —"what time will he come back?"

"You've heard about the Resurrection Morn,

20

haven't you, Minervy Ann?" There was a pious twang in the Major's voice as he pronounced the words.

"I hear de preacher say sump'n 'bout it," replied Aunt Minervy Ann.

"Well," said the Major, "along about that time Hamp will return. I hope his record is good enough to give him wings."

"Shuh! Marse Tumlin! you-all des fool'in' me. I don't keer—Hamp ain't gwine wid um. I tell you dat right now."

"Oh, he may not want to go," persisted the Major, "but he'll go all the same if they get their hands on him."

"My life er me!" exclaimed Aunt Minervy Ann, bristling up, "does you-all 'speck I'm gwine ter let um take Hamp out dat away? De fus' man come ter my door, less'n it's one er you-all, I'm gwine ter fling a pan er hot embers in his face ef de Lord'll gi' me de strenk. An' ef dat don't do no good, I'll scald um wid b'ilin' water. You hear dat, don't you?"

"Minervy Ann," said the Major, sweetly, "have you ever heard of the Ku-Klux?"

"Yasser, I is!" she exclaimed with startling emphasis. She stopped still and gazed hard at the Major. In response, he merely shrugged his shoulders

21

and raised his right hand with a swift gesture that told the whole story.

" Name er God! Marse Tumlin, is you an' Marse Bolivar and dish yer young genterman gwine ter set down here flat-footed and let dem Kukluckers scarify Hamp? "

" Why should *we* do anything? You've got everything arranged. You're going to singe 'em with hot embers, and you're going to take their hides off with scalding water. What more do you want? " The Major spoke with an air of benign resignation.

Aunt Minervy Ann shook her head vigorously. " Ef dey er de Kukluckers, fire won't do um no harm. Dey totes der haids in der han's."

" Their heads in their hands? " cried Colonel Blasengame, excitedly.

" Dat what dey say, suh," replied Aunt Minervy Ann.

Colonel Blasengame looked at his watch. " Tumlin, I'll have to ask you to excuse me to-night," he said. " I—well, the fact is, I have a mighty important engagement up town. I'm obliged to fill it." He turned to Aunt Minervy Ann: " Did I understand you to say the Ku-Klux carry their heads in their hands? "

"Dat what folks tell me. I hear my own color sesso," replied Aunt Minervy Ann.

"I'd be glad to stay with you, Tumlin," the Colonel declared; "but—well, under the circumstances, I think I'd better fill that engagement. Justice to my family demands it."

"Well," responded Major Perdue, "if you are going, I reckon we'd just as well go, too."

"Huh!" exclaimed Aunt Minervy Ann, "ef gwine's de word, dey can't nobody beat me gittin' way fum here. Dey may beat me comin' back, I ain't 'sputin' dat; but dey can't beat me gwine 'way. I'm ol', but I got mighty nigh ez much go in me ez a quarter-hoss."

Colonel Blasengame leaned back in his chair and studied the ceiling. "It seems to me, Tumlin, we might compromise on this. Suppose we get Hamp to come in here. Minervy Ann can stay out there in the kitchen and throw a rock against the back door when the Ku-Klux come."

Aunt Minervy Ann fairly gasped. "*Who? Me?* I'll die fust. I'll t'ar dat do' down; I'll holler twel ev'ybody in de neighborhood come a-runnin'. Ef you don't b'lieve me, you des try me. I'll paw up dat back-yard."

Major Perdue went to the back door and called

Hamp, but there was no answer. He called him a second time, with the same result.

" Well," said the Major, " they've stolen a march on us. They've come and carried him off while we were talking."

" No, suh, dey ain't, needer. I know right whar he is, an' I'm gwine atter 'im. He's right 'cross de street dar, colloguin' wid dat ol' Ceely Ensign. Dat's right whar he is."

"Old! Why, Celia is young," remarked the Major. " They say she's the best cook in town."

Aunt Minervy Ann whipped out of the room and was gone some little time. When she returned, she had Hamp with her, and I noticed that both were laboring under excitement which they strove in vain to suppress.

" Here I is, suh," said Hamp. " 'Nervy Ann say you call me."

" How is Celia to-night? " Colonel Blasengame inquired, suavely.

This inquiry, so suddenly and unexpectedly put, seemed to disconcert Hamp. He shuffled his feet and put his hand to his face. I noticed a blue welt over his eye, which was not there when he visited me in the afternoon.

" Well, suh, I 'speck she's tolerbul."

"*Is she? Is she? Ah-h-h!*" cried Aunt Minervy Ann.

"She must be pretty well," said the Major. "I see she's hit you a clip over the left eye."

"Dat's some er 'Nervy Ann's doin's, suh," replied Hamp, somewhat disconsolately.

"Den what you git in de way fer?" snapped Aunt Minervy Ann.

"Marse Tumlin, dat ar 'oman ain't done nothin' in de roun' worl'. She say she want me to buy some hime books fer de church when I went to Atlanty, an' I went over dar atter de money."

"*I himed 'er an' I churched 'er!*" exclaimed Aunt Minervy Ann.

"Here de money right here," said Hamp, pulling a small roll of shinplasters out of his pocket; "an' whiles we settin' dar countin' de money, 'Nervy Ann come in dar an' frail dat 'oman out."

"Ain't you hear dat nigger holler, Marse Tumlin?" inquired Minervy Ann. She was in high good-humor now. "Look like ter me dey could a-heerd 'er blate in de nex' county ef dey'd been a-lis'nin'. 'Twuz same ez a picnic, suh, an' I'm gwine 'cross dar 'fo' long an' pay my party call."

Then she began to laugh, and pretty soon went through the whole episode for our edification, dwelling with unction on that part where the unfortunate victim of her jealousy had called her "Miss 'Nervy." The more she laughed the more serious Hamp became.

At the proper time he was told of the visitation that was to be made by the Ku-Klux, and this information seemed to perplex and worry him no little. But his face lit up with genuine thankfulness when the programme for the occasion was announced to him. He and Minervy Ann were to remain in the house and not show their heads until the Major or the Colonel or their guest came to the back door and drummed on it lightly with the fingers.

Then the arms—three shot-guns—were brought out, and I noticed with some degree of surprise, that as the Major and the Colonel began to handle these, their spirits rose perceptibly. The Major hummed a tune and the Colonel whistled softly as they oiled the locks and tried the triggers. The Major, in coming home, had purchased four pounds of mustard-seed shot, and with this he proceeded to load two of the guns. In the third he placed only powder. This harmless weapon was intended for me, while the others were to be handled by Major Perdue and Colonel Blasengame. I learned afterward

In the third he placed only powder.

that the arrangement was made solely for my bene-fit. The Major and the Colonel were afraid that a young hand might become excited and fire too high at close range, in which event mustard-seed shot would be as dangerous as the larger variety.

At twelve o'clock I noticed that both Hamp and Aunt Minervy were growing restless.

" You hear dat clock, don't you, Marse Tum-lin? " said Minervy as the chimes died away. " Ef you don't min', de Kukluckers'll be a-stickin' dei haids in de back do'."

But the Major and the Colonel were playing a rubber of seven-up (or high-low-Jack) and paid no attention. It was a quarter after twelve when the game was concluded and the players pushed their chairs back from the table.

" Ef you don't fin' um in de yard waitin' fer you, I'll be fooled might'ly," remarked Aunt Minervy Ann.

" Go and see if they're out there," said the Major.

" *Me*, Marse Tumlin? *Me?* I wouldn't go out dat do' not for ham."

The Major took out his watch. " They'll eat and drink until twelve or a little after, and then they'll get ready to start. Then they'll have an-other drink all 'round, and finally they'll take another. It'll be a quarter to one or after when they get in the grove in the far end of the lot. But we'll go out now and see how the land lays. By the time they get here, our eyes will be used to the darkness."

The light was carried to a front room, and we groped our way out at the back door the best we could. The night was dark, but the stars were shining. I noticed that the belt and sword of Orion had drifted above the tree-tops in the east, following the Pleiades. In a little while the darkness seemed to grow less dense, and I could make out the outlines of trees twenty feet away.

Behind one of these trees, near the outhouse in which Hamp and Aunt Minervy lived, I was to take my stand, while the Major and the Colonel were to go farther into the wood-lot so as to greet the would-be Ku-Klux as they made their retreat, of which Major Perdue had not the slightest doubt.

"You stand here," said the Major in a whisper. "We'll go to the far-end of the lot where they're likely to come in. They'll pass us all right enough, but as soon as you see one of 'em, up with the gun an' lam aloose, an' before they can get away give 'em the other barrel. Then you'll hear from us."

Major Perdue and Colonel Blasengame disappeared in the darkness, leaving me, as it were, on

the inner picket line. I found the situation somewhat ticklish, as the saying is. There was not the
slightest danger, and I knew it, but if you ever have
occasion to stand out in the dark, waiting for something to happen, you'll find there's a certain degree
of suspense attached to it. And the loneliness and
silence of the night will take a shape almost tangi-
ble. The stirring of the half-dead leaves, the chirp-
ing of a belated cricket, simply emphasized the loneliness and made the silence more profound. At
intervals, all nature seemed to heave a deep sigh,
and address itself to slumber again.

In the house I heard the muffled sound of the
clock chime one, but whether it was striking the
half-hour or the hour I could not tell. Then I heard
the stealthy tread of feet. Someone stumbled over
a stick of timber, and the noise was followed by a
smothered exclamation and a confused murmur of
voices. As the story-writers say, I knew that the
hour had come. I could hear whisperings, and then
I saw a tall shadow steal from behind Aunt Minervy's house, and heard it rap gently on the door. I
raised the gun, pulled the hammer back, and let
drive. A stream of fire shot from the gun, accompanied by a report that tore the silence to atoms. I
heard a sharp exclamation of surprise, then the noise

of running feet, and off went the other barrel. In a moment the Major and the Colonel opened on the fugitives. I heard a loud cry of pain from one, and, in the midst of it all, the mustard-seed shot rattled on the plank fence like hominy-snow on a tin roof.

The next instant I heard someone running back in my direction, as if for dear life. He knew the place apparently, for he tried to go through the orchard, but just before he reached the orchard fence, he uttered a half-strangled cry of terror, and then I heard him fall as heavily as if he had dropped from the top of the house.

It was impossible to imagine what had happened, and it was not until we had investigated the matter that the cause of the trouble was discovered. A wire clothes-line, stretched across the yard, had caught the would-be Ku-Klux under the chin, his legs flew from under him, and he had a fall, from the effects of which he was long in recovering. He was a young man about town, very well connected, who had gone into the affair in a spirit of mischief. We carried him into the house, and administered to his hurts the best we could; Aunt Minervy Ann, be it said to her credit, being more active in this direction than any of us.

On the Tuesday following, the county paper contained the news in a form that remains to this day unique. It is hardly necessary to say that it was from the pen of Major Tumlin Perdue.

"Last Saturday afternoon our local editor was informed by a prominent citizen that if he would apply to Major Perdue he would be put in possession of a very interesting piece of news. Acting upon this hint, ye local yesterday went to Major Perdue, who, being in high good-humor, wrote out the following with his own hand:

"'Late Saturday night, while engaged with a party of friends in searching for a stray dog on my premises, I was surprised to see four or five men climb over my back fence and proceed toward my residence. As my most intimate friends do not visit me by climbing over my back fence, I immediately deployed my party in such a manner as to make the best of a threatening situation. The skirmish opened at my kitchen-door, with two rounds from a howitzer. This demoralized the enemy, who promptly retreated the way they came. One of them, the leader of the attacking party, carried away with him two loads of mustard-seed shot, delivered in the general neighborhood and region of the coat-tails, which, being on a level with the horizon, afforded as fair a target as could be had in the dark.

31

I understand on good authority that Mr. Larry Pulliam, one of our leading and deservedly popular citizens, has had as much as a quart of mustard-seed shot picked from his carcass. Though hit in a vulnerable spot, the wound is not mortal.—T. PERDUE.' "

I did my best to have Mr. Pulliam's name suppressed, but the Major would not have it so.

" No, sir," he insisted; " the man has insulted me behind my back, and he's got to cut wood or put down the axe."

Naturally this free and easy card created quite a sensation in Halcyondale and the country round about. People knew what it would mean if Major Perdue's name had been used in such an off-hand manner by Mr. Pulliam, and they naturally supposed that a fracas would be the outcome. Public expectation was on tiptoe, and yet the whole town seemed to take the Major's card humorously. Some of the older citizens laughed until they could hardly sit up, and even Mr. Pulliam's friends caught the infection. Indeed, it is said that Mr. Pulliam, himself, after the first shock of surprise was over, paid the Major's audacious humor the tribute of a hearty laugh. When Mr. Pulliam appeared in public, among the first men he saw was Major Perdue. This

"I'd a heap rather you'd pull your shot-gun on me than your pen."

was natural, for the Major made it a point to be on hand. He was not a ruffler, but he thought it was his duty to give Mr. Pulliam a fair opportunity to wreak vengeance on him. If the boys about town imagined that a row was to be the result of this first meeting, they were mistaken. Mr. Pulliam looked at the Major and then began to laugh.

"Major Perdue," he said, "I'd a heap rather you'd pull your shot-gun on me than your pen."

And that ended the matter.

II

"WHEN JESS WENT A-FIDDLIN'"

The foregoing recital is unquestionably a long and tame preface to the statement that, after thinking the matter over I concluded to accept the official invitation to the fair—"The Middle Georgia Exposition" it was called—if nothing occurred to prevent. With this conclusion I dismissed the matter from my mind for the time being, and would probably have thought of it no more until the moment arrived to make a final decision, if the matter had not been called somewhat sharply to my attention.

Sitting on the veranda one day, ruminating over other people's troubles, I heard an unfamiliar voice calling, " You-all got any bitin' dogs here?" The voice failed to match the serenity of the suburban scene. Its tone was pitched a trifle too high for the surroundings.

But before I could make any reply the gate was flung open, and the new-comer, who was no other than Aunt Minervy Ann, flirted in and began to climb the terraces. My recognition of her was not immediate, partly because it had been long since I saw her and partly because she wore her Sunday toggery, in which, following the oriental tastes of her race, the reds and yellows were emphasized with startling effect. She began to talk by the time she was half-way between the house and gate, and it was owing to this special and particular volubility that I was able to recognize her.

" Huh! " she exclaimed, " hit's des like clim'in' up sta'rs. Folks what live here bleeze ter b'long ter de Sons er Tempunce." There was a relish about this reference to the difficulties of three terraces that at once identified Aunt Minervy Ann. More than that, one of the most conspicuous features of the country town where she lived was a large brick building, covering half a block, across the top of which stretched a sign—" Temperance Hall "—in letters that could be read half a mile away.

Aunt Minervy Ann received a greeting that seemed to please her, whereupon she explained that an excursion had come to Atlanta from her town, and she had seized the opportunity to pay me a visit. " I tol' um," said she, " dat dey could stay up in town dar an' hang 'roun' de kyar-shed ef dey wanter, but here's what wuz gwine ter come out an' see whar you live at, an' fin' out fer Marse Tumlin ef you comin' down ter de fa'r.''

She was informed that, though she was welcome, she would get small pleasure from her visit. The cook had failed to make her appearance, and the lady of the house was at that moment in the kitchen and in a very fretful state of mind, not because she had to cook, but because she had about reached the point where she could place no dependence in the sisterhood of colored cooks.

" Is she in de kitchen now? " Aunt Minervy's tone was a curious mixture of amusement and indignation. " I started not ter come, but I had a call, I sho' did; sump'n tol' me dat you mought need me out here." With that, she went into the house, slamming the screen-door after her, and untying her bonnet as she went.

Now, the lady of the house had heard of Aunt Minervy Ann, but had never met her, and I was afraid that the characteristics of my old-time friend would be misunderstood and misinterpreted. The lady in question knew nothing of the negro race until long after emancipation, and she had not been able to form a very favorable opinion of its representatives. Therefore, I hastened after Aunt Minervy Ann, hoping to tone down by explanation whatever bad impression she might create. She paused at the screen-door that barred the entrance to the kitchen, and, for an instant, surveyed the scene within. Then she cried out:

" You des ez well ter come out'n dat kitchen! You ain't got no mo' bizness in dar dan a new-born baby."

Aunt Minervy Ann's voice was so loud and absolute that the lady gazed at her in mute astonishment. " You des es well ter come out! " she insisted.

" Are you crazy? " the lady asked, in all seriousness.

" I'm des ez crazy now ez I ever been; an' I tell you you des ez well ter come out'n dar."

". Who are you anyhow? "

" I'm Minervy Ann Perdue, at home an' abroad, an' in dish yer great town whar you can't git niggers ter cook fer you."

" Well, if you want me to come out of the kitchen, you will have to come in and do the cooking."

" Dat 'zackly what I'm gwine ter do! " exclaimed Aunt Minervy Ann. She went into the kitchen, demanded an apron, and took entire charge. " I'm mighty glad I come 'fo' you got started," she said, " 'kaze you got 'nuff fier in dis stove fer ter barbecue a hoss; an' you got it so hot in here dat it's a wonder you ain't bust a blood-vessel."

She removed all the vessels from the range, and opened the door of the furnace so that the fire might die down. And when it was nearly out—as I was told afterward—she replaced the vessels and proceeded to cook a dinner which, in all its characteristics, marked a red letter day in the household.

" She's the best cook in the country," said the lady, " and she's not very polite."

" Not very hypocritical, you mean; well if she was a hypocrite, she wouldn't be Aunt Minervy Ann."

The cook failed to come in the afternoon, and so Aunt Minervy Ann felt it her duty to remain over night. " Hamp'll vow I done run away wid somebody," she said, laughing, " but I don't keer what he think."

After supper, which was as good as the dinner had been, Aunt Minervy Ann came out on the veranda and sat on the steps. After some conversation, she placed the lady of the house on the witness-stand.

" Mistiss, wharbouts in Georgy wuz you born at?"

" I wasn't born in Georgia; I was born in Lansingburgh, New York."

"I know'd it!" Aunt Minervy turned to me and nodded her head with energy. "I know'd it right pine blank!"

"You knew what?" the presiding genius of the household inquired with some curiosity.

"I know'd 'm dat you wuz a Northron lady."

"I don't see how you knew it," I remarked.

"Well, suh, she talk like we-all do, an' she got mighty much de same ways. But when I went out dar dis mornin' an' holler at 'er in de kitchen, I know'd by de way she turn 'roun' on me dat she ain't been brung up wid niggers. Ef she'd 'a' been a Southron lady, she'd 'a' laughed an' said, ' Come in here an' cook dis dinner yo'se'f, you ole vilyun,' er she'd 'a' come out an' crackt me over de head with dat i'on spoon what she had in her han'."

I could perceive a vast amount of acuteness in the observation, but I said nothing, and, after a considerable pause, Aunt Minervy Ann remarked:

"Dey er lots er mighty good folks up dar "—indicating the North—" some I've seed wid my own eyes an' de yuthers I've heern talk un. Mighty fine folks, an' dey say dey mighty sorry fer de niggers. But I'll tell um all anywhar, any day, dat I'd lots druther dey'd be good ter me dan ter be sorry fer me. You know dat ar white lady what Marse

39

Tom Chippendale married? Her pa come down here ter he'p de niggers, an' he done it de best he kin, but Marse Tom's wife can't b'ar de sight un um. She won't let um go in her kitchen, she won't let um go in her house, an' she don't want um nowhars 'roun'. She's mighty sorry fer 'm, but she don't like um. I don't blame 'er much myse'f, bekaze it look like dat de niggers what been growin' up sence freedom is des tryin' der han' fer ter see how no 'count dey kin be. Dey'll git better—dey er bleeze ter git better, 'kaze dey can't git no wuss."

Here came another pause, which continued until Aunt Minervy Ann, turning her head toward me, asked if I knew the lady that Jesse Towers married; and before I had time to reply with certainty, she went on:

"No, suh, you des can't know 'er. She ain't come dar twel sev'mty, an' I mos' know you ain't see 'er dat time you went down home de las' time, 'kaze she wa'n't gwine out dat year. Well, she wuz a Northron lady. I come mighty nigh tellin' you 'bout 'er when you wuz livin' dar, but fus' one thing an' den anudder jumped in de way; er maybe 'twuz too new ter be goshup'd 'roun' right den. But de way she come ter be dar an' de way it all turn out beats any er dem tales what de ol' folks use ter tell we childun. I may not know all de ins an' outs, but what I does know I knows mighty well, 'kaze de young 'oman tol' me herse'f right out 'er own mouf.

"Fus' an' fo'mus', dar wuz ol' Gabe Towers. He wuz dar whence you wuz dar, an' long time 'fo' dat. You know'd him, sho', 'kaze he wuz one er dem kinder men what sticks out fum de res' like a waggin' tongue. Not dat he wuz any better'n anybody else, but he had dem kinder ways what make folks talk 'bout 'im an' 'pen' on 'im. I dunner 'zackly what de ways wuz, but I knows dat whatsomever ol' Gabe Towers say an' do, folks 'd nod der head an' say an' do de same. An' me 'long er de res'. He had dem kinder ways 'bout 'im, an' 'twa'n't no use talkin'."

In these few words, Aunt Minervy conjured up in my mind the memory of one of the most remarkable men I had ever known. He was tall, with iron-gray hair. His eyes were black and brilliant, his nose slightly curved, and his chin firm without heaviness. To this day Gabriel Towers stands out in my admiration foremost among all the men I have ever known. He might have been a great statesman; he would have been great in anything to which he turned his hand. But he contented himself with instructing smaller men, who were merely politicians, and with sowing and reaping on his plantation. More than one senator went to him for ideas with which to make a reputation.

His will seemed to dominate everybody with whom he came in contact, not violently, but serenely and surely, and as a matter of course. Whether this was due to his age—he was sixty-eight when I knew him, having been born in the closing year of the eighteenth century—or to his moral power, or to his personal magnetism, it is hardly worth while to inquire. Major Perdue said that the secret of his influence was common-sense, and this is perhaps as good an explanation as any. The immortality of Socrates and Plato should be enough to convince us that common-sense is almost as inspiring as the gift of prophecy. To interpret Aunt Minervy Ann in this way is merely to give a correct report of what occurred on the veranda, for explanation of this kind was necessary to give the lady of the house something like a familiar interest in the recital.

" Yes, suh," Aunt Minervy Ann went on, " he had dem kinder ways 'bout 'im, an' whatsomever he say you can't shoo it off like you would a hen on de gyarden fence. Dar 'twuz an' dar it stayed.

" Well, de time come when ol' Marse Gabe had

a gran'son, an' he name 'im Jesse in 'cordance wid
de Bible. Jesse grow'd an' grow'd twel he got ter
be a right smart chunk uv a boy, but he wa'n't no
mo' like de Towerses dan he wuz like de Chippendales, which he wa'n't no kin to. He tuck atter his
ma, an' who his ma tuck atter I'll never tell you,
'kaze Bill Henry Towers married 'er way off yander
somers. She wuz purty but puny, yit puny ez she
wuz she could play de peanner by de hour, an' play
it mo' samer de man what make it.

" Well, suh, Jesse tuck atter his ma in looks, but
'stidder playin' de peanner, he l'arnt how ter play de
fiddle, an' by de time he wuz twelve year ol', he
could make it talk. Hit's de fatal trufe, suh; he
could make it talk. You hear folks playin' de fiddle,
an' you know what dey doin'; you kin hear de
strings a-plunkin' an' you kin hear de bow raspin' on
um on 'count de rozzum, but when Jesse Towers
swiped de bow cross his fiddle, 'twa'n't no fiddle—
'twuz human; I ain't tellin' you no lie, suh, 'twuz
human. Dat chile could make yo' heart ache; he
could fetch yo' sins up befo' you. Don't tell me!
many an' many a night when I hear Jesse Towers
playin', I could shet my eyes an' hear my childun
cryin', dem what been dead an' buried long time
ago. Don't make no diffunce 'bout de chune, reel,

43

jig, er promenade, de human cryin' wuz behime all un um.

"Bimeby, Jesse got so dat he didn't keer nothin' 'tall 'bout books. It uz fiddle, fiddle, all day long, an' half de night ef dey'd let 'im. Den folks 'gun ter talk. No need ter tell you what all dey say. De worl' over, fum what I kin hear, dey got de idee dat a fiddle is a free pass ter whar ole Scratch live at. Well, suh, Jesse got so he'd run away fum school an' go off in de woods an' play his fiddle. Hamp use ter come 'pon 'im when he haulin' wood, an' he say dat fiddle ain't soun' no mo' like de fiddles what you hear in common dan a flute soun' like a bass drum.

"Now you know yo'se'f, suh, dat dis kinder doin's ain't gwine ter suit Marse Gabe Towers. Time he hear un it, he put his foot down on fiddler, an' fiddle, an' fiddlin'. Ez you may say, he sot down on de fiddle an' smash it. Dis happen when Jesse wuz sixteen year ol', an' by dat time he wuz mo' in love wid de fiddle dan what he wuz wid his gran'daddy. An' so dar 'twuz. He ain't look like it, but Jesse wuz about ez high strung ez his fiddle wuz, an' when his gran'daddy laid de law down, he sol' out his pony an' buggy an' made his disappearance fum dem parts.

"Well, suh, 'twa'n't so mighty often you'd hear

sassy talk 'bout Marse Gabe Towers, but you could hear it den. Folks is allers onreasonable wid dem dey like de bes'; you know dat yo'se'f, suh. Marse Gabe ain't make no 'lowance fer Jesse, an' folks ain't make none fer Marse Gabe. Marse Tumlin wuz dat riled wid de man dat dey come mighty nigh havin' a fallin' out. Dey had a splutter 'bout de time when sump'n n'er had happen, an' atter dey wrangle a little, Marse Tumlin sot de date by sayin' dat 'twuz ' a year 'fo' de day when Jess went a-fiddlin'.' Dat sayin' kindled de fier, suh, an' it spread fur an' wide. Marse Tom Chippendale say dat folks what never is hear tell er de Towerses went 'roun' talkin' 'bout ' de time when Jess went a-fiddlin'.' "

Aunt Minervy Ann chuckled over this, probably because she regarded it as a sort of victory for Major Tumlin Perdue. She went on:

" Yes, suh, 'twuz a by-word wid de childun. No matter what happen, er when it happen, er ef 'tain't happen, 'twuz 'fo' er atter ' de day when Jess went a-fiddlin'.' Hit look like dat Marse Gabe sorter drapt a notch or two in folks' min's. Yit he helt his head dez ez high. He bleeze ter hol' it high, 'kaze he had in 'im de blood uv bofe de Tumlins an' de Perdues; I dunner how much, but 'nuff fer ter keep his head up.

"I ain't no almanac, suh, but I never is ter fergit de year when Jess went a-fiddlin. 'Twuz sixty, 'kaze de nex' year de war 'gun ter bile, an' 'twa'n't long 'fo' it biled over. Yes, suh! dar wuz de war come on an Jess done gone. Dey banged aloose, dey did, dem on der side, an' we on our'n, an' dey kep' on a bangin' twel we-all can't bang no mo'. An' den de war hushed up, an' freedom come, an' still nobody ain't hear tell er Jesse. Den you come down dar, suh, an' stay what time you did; still nobody ain't hear tell er Jesse. He mought er writ ter his ma, but ef he did, she kep' it mighty close. Marse Gabe ain't los' no flesh 'bout it, an' ef he los' any sleep on account er Jess, he ain't never brag 'bout it.

" Well, suh, it went on dis away twel, ten year atter Jess went a-fiddlin', his wife come home. Yes, suh! His wife! Well! I wuz stan'in' right in de hall talkin' wid Miss Fanny—dat's Jesse's ma— when she come, an' when de news broke on me you could 'a' knockt me down wid a permeter fan. De house-gal show'd 'er in de parler, an' den come atter Miss Fanny. Miss Fanny she went in dar, an' I stayed outside talkin' wid de house-gal. De gal say, ' Aunt Minervy Ann, dey sho' is sump'n n'er de matter wid dat white lady. She white ez any er de dead, an' she can't git 'er breff good.' 'Bout dat

46

time, I hear somebody cry out in de parler, an' den I hear sump'n fall. De house-gal cotch holt er me an' 'gun ter whimper. I shuck 'er off, I did, an' went right straight in de parler, an' dar wuz Miss Fanny layin' face fo'mus' on a sofy wid a letter in 'er han' an' de white lady sprawled out on de flo'.

" Well, suh, you can't skeer me wid trouble 'kaze I done see too much; so I shuck Miss Fanny by de arm an' ax 'er what de matter, an' she cry out, ' Jesse's dead an' his wife come home.' She uz plum heart-broke, suh, an' I 'speck I wuz blubberin' some myse'f when Marse Gabe walkt in, but I wuz tryin' ter work wid de white lady on de flo'. 'Twix' Marse Gabe an' Miss Fanny, 'twuz sho'ly a tryin' time. When one er dem hard an' uppity men lose der grip on deyse'f, dey turn loose ever'thing, an' dat wuz de way wid Marse Gabe. When dat de case, sump'n n'er got ter be done, an' it got ter be done mighty quick."

Aunt Minervy Ann paused here and rubbed her hands together contemplatively, as if trying to restore the scene more completely to her memory.

" You know how loud I kin talk, suh, when I'm min' ter. Well, I talk loud den an' dar. I 'low, ' What you-all doin'? Is you gwine ter let Marse Jesse's wife lay here an' die des 'kaze he dead? Ef you is, I'll des go whar I b'longs at!' Dis kinder fotch um 'roun', an' 'twa'n't no time 'fo' we had de white lady in de bed whar Jesse use ter sleep at, an' soon's we got 'er cuddled down in it, she come 'roun'. But she wuz in a mighty bad fix. She wanter git up an' go off, an' 'twuz all I could do fer ter keep 'er in bed. She done like she wuz plum distracted. Dey wa'n't skacely a minnit fer long hours, an' dey wuz mighty long uns, suh, dat she wa'n't moanin' an' sayin' dat she wa'n't gwine ter stay, an' she hope de Lord'd fergive 'er. I tell you, suh, 'twuz tarryfyin'. I shuck nex' day des like folks do when dey er honin' atter dram.

"You may ax me how come I ter stay dar," Aunt Minervy Ann suggested with a laugh. "Well, suh, 'twa'n't none er my doin's. I 'speck dey mus' be sump'n wrong 'bout me, 'kaze no matter how rough I talk ner how ugly I look, sick folks an' childun allers takes up wid me. When I go whar dey is, it's mighty hard fer ter git 'way fum um. So, when I say ter Jesse's wife, 'Keep still, honey, an' I'll go home an' not pester you,' she sot up in bed an' say ef I gwine she gwine too. I say, 'Nummine 'bout me, honey, you lay down dar an' don't talk too much.' She 'low, 'Le' me talk ter you an' tell you all 'bout it.' But I shuck my head an' say dat ef she don't hush up an' keep still I'm gwine right home.

"I had ter do 'er des like she wuz a baby, suh. She wa'n't so mighty purty, but she had purty ways, 'stracted ez she wuz, an' de biggest black eyes you mos' ever seed, an' black curly ha'r cut short kinder, like our folks use ter w'ar der'n. Den de house-gal fotched some tea an' toas', an' dis holp 'er up might-ly, an' atter dat I sont ter Marse Gabe fer some dram, an' de gal fotched de decanter fum de side-bode. Bein', ez you may say, de nurse, I tuck an' tas'e er de dram fer ter make sho' dat nobody ain't put nothin' in it. An', sho' 'nuff, dey ain't."

Aunt Minervy Ann paused and smacked her lips. "Atter she got de vittles an' de dram, she sorter drap off ter sleep, but 'twuz a mighty flighty kinder sleep. She'd wake wid a jump des 'zackly like ba-bies does, an' den she'd moan an' worry twel she dozed off ag'in. I nodded, suh, bekaze you can't set me down in a cheer, night er day, but what I'll nod, but in betwix' an' betweens I kin hear Marse Gabe Towers walkin' up an' down in de liberry; walk, walk; walk, walk, up an' down. I 'speck ef I'd 'a' been one er de nervious an' flighty kin' dey'd 'a' had to tote me out er dat house de nex' day; but me! I des kep' on a-noddin'.

49

" Bimeby, I hear sump'n come swishin' 'long, an' in walkt Miss Fanny. I tell you now, suh, ef I'd a met 'er comin' down de road, I'd 'a' made a break fer de bushes, she look so much like you know sperrets oughter look—an' Marse Jesse's wife wuz layin' dar wid 'er eyes wide open. She sorter swunk back in de bed when she see Miss Fanny, an' cry out, ' Oh, I'm mighty sorry fer ter trouble you; I'm gwine 'way in de mornin'.' Miss Fanny went ter de bed an' knelt down 'side it, an' 'low, ' No, you ain't gwine no whar but right in dis house. Yo' place is here, wid his mudder an' his gran'fadder.' Wid dat, Marse Jesse's wife put her face in de piller an' moan an' cry, twel I hatter ax Miss Fanny fer ter please, ma'm, go git some res'.

" Well, suh, I stayed dar dat night an part er de nex' day, an' by dat time all un um wuz kinder quieted down, but dey wuz mighty res'less in de min', 'speshually Marse Jesse's wife, which her name wuz Miss Sadie. It seem like dat Marse Jesse wuz livin' at a town up dar in de fur North whar dey wuz a big lake, an' he went out wid one er dem 'scursion parties, an' a storm come up an' shuck de boat ter pieces. Dat what make I say what I does. I don't min' gwine on 'scursions on de groun', but when it come ter water—well, suh, I ain't gwine ter

50

trus' myse'f on water twel I kin walk on it an' not
wet my foots. Marse Jesse wuz de Captain uv a
music-ban' up dar, an' de papers fum dar had some
long pieces 'bout 'im, an' de paper at home had a
piece 'bout 'im. It say he wuz one er de mos' re-
nounced music-makers what yever had been, an' dat
when it come ter dat kinder doin's he wuz a puffick
prodigal. I 'member de words, suh, bekaze I made
Hamp read de piece out loud mo' dan once.

" Miss Sadie, she got mo' calmer atter while, an'
'twa'n't long 'fo' Marse Gabe an' Miss Fanny wuz
bofe mighty tuck up wid 'er. Dey much'd 'er up
an' made a heap un 'er, an' she fa'rly hung on dem.
I done tol' you she ain't purty, but dey wuz sump'n
'bout 'er better dan purtiness. It mought er been 'er
eyes, en den ag'in mought er been de way er de gal;
but whatsomever 'twuz, hit made you think 'bout
'er at odd times durin' de day, an' des 'fo' you go ter
sleep at night.

" Eve'ything went swimmin' along des ez natchul
ez a duck floatin' on de mill-pon'. Dey wa'n't skacely a day but what I seed Miss Sadie. Ef I ain't go
ter Marse Gabe's house she'd be sho' ter come ter
mine. Dat uz atter Hamp wuz 'lected ter de legislatur, suh. He 'low dat a member er de ingener'l
ensembly ain't got no bizness livin' in a kitchen, but

I say he ain't a whit better den dan he wuz befo'.
So be, I done been cross 'im so much dat I tell 'im
ter git de house an' I'd live in it ef 'twa'n't too fur
fum Miss Vallie an' Marse Tumlin. Well, he had it
built on de outskyirts, not a big jump fum Miss Vallie an' betwix' de town an' Marse Gabe Towers's.
When you come down ter de fa'r, you mus' come
see me. Me an' Hamp'll treat you right; we sholy
will.

" Well, suh, in dem days dey wa'n't so many niggers willin' ter do an' be done by, an' on account er
dat, ef Miss Vallie wa'n't hollin' fer 'Nervy Ann,
Miss Fanny er Miss Sadie wuz, an' when I wa'n't at
one place, you might know I'd be at de yuther one.
It went on dis away, an' went on twel one day got so
much like an'er dat you can't tell Monday fum Friday. An' it went on an' went on twel bimeby I wuz
bleeze ter say sump'n ter Hamp. You take notice,
suh, an' when you see de sun shinin' nice an' warm
an' de win' blowin' so saft an' cool dat you wanter
go in a-washin' in it—when you see dis an' feel dat
away, *Watch out! Watch out*, I tell you! Dat des
de time when de harrycane gwine ter come up out'n
de middle er de swamp an' t'ar things ter tatters.
Same way when folks gitting on so nice dat dey
don't know dey er gittin' on.

"De fus' news I know'd Miss Sadie wuz bringin' little bundles ter my house 'twix' sundown an' dark. She'd 'low, ' Aunt Minervy Ann, I'll des put dis in de cornder here; I may want it some time.' Nex' day it'd be de same doin's over ag'in. ' Aunt Minervy Ann, please take keer er dis; I may want it some time.' Well, it went on dis away fum day ter day, but I ain't pay no 'tention. Ef any 'spicion cross my min' it wuz dat maybe Miss Sadie puttin' dem things dar fer ter 'sprise me Chris'mus by tellin' me dey wuz fer me. But one day she come ter my house, an' sot down an' put her han's over her face like she got de headache er sump'n.

"Wellum "—Aunt Minervy Ann, with real tact, now began to address herself to the lady of the house —" Wellum, she sot dar so long dat bimeby I ax 'er what de matter is. She ain't say nothin'; she ain't make no motion. I 'low ter myse'f dat she don't wanter be pestered, so I let 'er 'lone an' went on 'bout my business. But, bless you! de nex' time I look at 'er she wuz settin' des dat away wid 'er han's over her face. She sot so still dat it sorter make me feel quare, an' I went, I did, an' cotch holt er her han's sorter playful-like. Wellum, de way dey felt made me flinch. All I could say wuz, ' Lord 'a' mercy! ' She tuck her han's down, she did, an' look

53

at me an' smile kinder faint-like. She 'low, ' Wuz
my han's col', Aunt Minervy Ann?' I look at 'er
an' grunt, 'Huh! dey won't be no colder when
youer dead.' She ain't say nothin', an' terreckly I
'low, ' What de name er goodness is de matter wid
you, Miss Sadie?' She say, ' Nothin' much. I'm
gwine ter stay here ter-night, an' ter-morrer mornin'
I'm gwine 'way.' I ax 'er, ' How come dat? What
is dey done to you?' She say, ' Nothin' 'tall.' I
'low, ' Does Marse Gabe an' Miss Fanny know you
gwine? She say, ' No; I can't tell um.'

"Wellum, I flopt down on a cheer; yessum, I
sho' did. My min' wuz gwine like a whirligig an'
my head wuz swimmin'. I des sot dar an' look at
'er. Bimeby she up an' say, pickin' all de time at
her frock, ' I know'd sump'n wuz gwine ter happen.
Dat de reason I been bringin' dem bundles here.
In dem ar bundles you'll fin' all de things I fotch
here. I ain't got nothin' dey give me 'cep'n dish
yer black dress I got on. I'd 'a' fotche my ol' trunk,
but I dunner what dey done wid it. Hamp'll hatter
buy me one an' pay for it hisse'f, 'kaze I ain't got a
cent er money.' Dem de ve'y words she say. I
'low, ' Sump'n must 'a' happen den.' She nodded,
an' bimeby she say, ' Mr. Towers comin' home ter-
night. Dey done got a telegraph fum 'im.'

"I stood up in de flo', I did, an' ax 'er, 'Which Mr. Towers?' She say, 'Mr. Jesse Towers.' I 'low, 'He done dead.' She say, 'No, he ain't; ef he wuz he done come ter life; dey done got a telegraph fum 'im, I tell you.' 'Is *dat* de reason you gwine 'way?' I des holla'd it at 'er. She draw'd a long breff an' say, 'Yes, dat's de reason.'

"I tell you right now, ma'm, I didn't know ef I wuz stannin' on my head er floatin' in de a'r. I wuz plum outdone. But dar she sot des es cool ez a cur-cumber wid de dew on it. I went out de do', I did, an' walk 'roun' de house once ter de right an' twice ter de lef' bekaze de ol' folks use ter tell me dat ef you wuz bewitched, dat 'ud take de spell away. I ain't tellin' you no lie, ma'm—fer de longes' kinder minnit I didn't no mo' b'lieve dat Miss Sadie wuz settin' dar in my house tellin' me dat kinder riga-marole, dan I b'lieve I'm flyin' right now. Dat bein' de case, I bleeze ter fall back on bewitchments, an' so I walk 'roun' de house. But when I went back in, dar she wuz, settin' in a cheer an' lookin' up at de rafters.

"Wellum, I went in an' drapt down in a cheer an' lookt at 'er. Bimeby, I say, 'Miss Sadie, does you mean ter set dar an' tell me youer gwine 'way 'kaze yo' husban' comin' home?' She flung her

arms behime 'er head, she did, an' say, ' I ain't none
er his wife; I des been playin' off! ' De way she
look an' de way she say it wuz 'nuff fer me. I wuz
pairlized; yessum, I wuz dumfounder'd. Ef anybody had des but totch me wid de tip er der finger,
I'd 'a' fell off'n dat cheer an' never stirred atter I
hit de flo'. Ever'thing 'bout de house lookt quare.
Miss Vallie had a lookin'-glass one time wid de pictur' uv a church at de bottom. When de glass got
broke, she gimme de pictur', an' I sot it up on de
mantel-shelf. I never know'd 'fo' dat night dat de
steeple er der church wuz crooked. But dar 'twuz.
Mo' dan dat I cotch myse'f feelin' er my fingers fer
ter see ef 'twuz me an' ef I wuz dar.

" Talk 'bout *dreams!* dey wa'n't no dream could
beat dat, I don't keer how twisted it mought be.
An' den, ma'm, she sot back dar an' tol' me de whole
tale 'bout how she come ter be dar. I'll never tell it
like she did; dey ain't nobody in de wide worl' kin
do dat. But it seem like she an' Marse Jesse wuz
stayin' in de same neighborhoods, er stayin' at de
same place, he a-fiddlin' an' she a-knockin' on de
peanner er de harp, I fergit which. Anyhow, dey
seed a heap er one an'er. Bofe un um had come dar
fum way off yan', an' ain't got nobody but deyse'f
fer ter 'pen' on, an' dat kinder flung um togedder.

I 'speck dey must er swapt talk 'bout love an' mar-
ryin'—you know yo'se'f, ma'm, dat dat's de way
young folks is. Howsomever dat may be, Marse
Jesse, des ter tease 'er, sot down one day an' writ a
long letter ter his wife. Tooby sho' he ain't got no
wife, but he des make out he got one, an' dat letter
he lef' layin' 'roun' whar Miss Sadie kin see it.
'Twa'n't in no envelyup, ner nothin', an' you know
mighty well, ma'm, dat when a 'oman, young er ol',
see dat kinder letter layin' 'roun' she'd die ef she
don't read it. Fum de way Miss Sadie talk, dat letter must 'a' stirred up a coolness 'twix' um, kaze de
mornin' when he wuz gwine on dat 'scursion, Marse
Jesse pass by de place whar she wuz settin' at an'
flung de letter in her lap an' say, ' What's in dar wuz
fer you.'

" Wellum, wid dat he wuz gone, an' de fus' news
Miss Sadie know'd de papers wuz full er de names
er dem what got drownded in de boat, an' Marse
Jesse head de roll, 'kaze he wuz de mos' pop'lous
music-maker in de whole settlement. Den dar wuz
de gal an' de letter. I wish I could tell dis part like
she tol' me settin' dar in my house. You'll never git
it straight in yo' head less'n you'd 'a' been dar an'
hear de way she tol' it. Nigger ez I is, I know
mighty well dat a white 'oman ain't got no business

57

parmin' 'erse'f off ez a man's wife. But de way she
tol' it tuck all de rough aidges off'n it. She wuz dar
in dat big town, wuss'n a wilderness, ez you may
say, by 'erse'f, nobody 'penin' on 'er an' nobody
ter 'pen' on, tired down an' plum wo' out, an' wid
all dem kinder longin's what you know yo'se'f,
ma'am, all wimmen bleeze ter have, ef dey er white
er ef dey er black.

"Yit she ain't never tol' nobody dat she wuz Marse
Jesse's wife. She des han' de letter what she'd kep'
ter Miss Fanny, an' fell down on de flo' in a dead
faint, an' she say dat ef it hadn't but 'a' been fer me,
she'd a got out er de bed dat fust night an' went
'way fum dar; an' I know dat's so, too, bekaze she
wuz ranklin' fer ter git up fum dar. But at de time
I put all dat down ter de credit er de deleeriums, an'
made 'er stay in bed.

"Wellum, ef I know'd all de books in de worl'
by heart, I couldn't tell you how I felt atter she
done tol' me dat tale. She sot back dar des ez calm
ez a baby. Bimeby she say, ' I'm glad I tol' you;
I feel better dan I felt in a mighty long time.' It
look like, ma'am, dat a load done been lift fum 'er
min'. Now I know'd pine blank dat sump'n gotter
be done, 'kaze de train'd be in at midnight, an'
den when Marse Jesse come dey'd be a tarrifyin'

time at Gabe Towers's. Atter while I up an' ax 'er,
'Miss Sadie, did you reely love Marse Jesse?' She
say, 'Yes, I did'—des so. I ax 'er, 'Does you love
'im now?' She say, 'Yes, I does—an' I love dem
ar people up dar at de house; dat de reason I'm
gwine 'way.' She talk right out; she done come to
de p'int whar she ain't got nothin' ter hide.

"I say, 'Well, Miss Sadie, dem folks up at de
house, dey loves you.' She sorter flincht at dis.
I 'low, 'Dey been mighty good ter you. What
you done, you done done, an' dat can't be holp, but
what you ain't gone an' done, dat kin be holp; an'
what you oughter do, dat oughtn't ter be holp.' I
see 'er clinch 'er han's an' den I riz fum de
cheer." Suiting the action to the word, Aunt
Minervy Ann rose from the step where she had
been sitting, and moved toward the lady of the
house.

"I riz, I did, an' tuck my stan' befo' 'er. I 'low,
'You say you love Marse Jesse, an' you say you love
his folks. Well, den ef you got any blood in you,
ef you got any heart in yo' body, ef you got any
feelin' fer anybody in de roun' worl' 'cep'n' yo'
naked se'f, you'll go up dar ter dat house an' tell
Gabe Towers dat you want ter see 'im, an' you'll tell
Fanny Towers dat you want ter see her, an' you'll

59

stan' up befo' um an' tell um de tale you tol' ter me,
word fer word. Ef you'll do dat, an' you hatter
come back here, *come! come!* Bless God! *come!*
an' me an' Hamp'll rake an' scrape up 'nuff money
fer ter kyar you whar you gwine. An' don't you be
a'skeer'd er Gabe Towers. Me an' Marse Tumlin
ain't a-skeer'd un 'im. I'm gwine wid you, an' ef he
say one word out de way, you des come ter de do'
an' call me, an' ef I don't preach his funer'l, it'll be
bekaze de Lord'll strike me dumb!' *An' she
went!*"

Aunt Minervy paused. She had wrought the
miracle of summoning to life one of the crises
through which she had passed with others. It was
not the words she used. There was nothing in
them to stir the heart or quicken the pulse. Her
power lay in the tones of her voice, whereby she was
able to recall the passion of a moment that had long
spent itself; in the fluent and responsive attitudes;
in gesticulation that told far more than her words
did. The light from the vestibule lamp shone full
upon her and upon the lady whom she unconsciously
selected to play the part of the young woman whose
story she was telling. The illusion was perfect.
We were in Aunt Minervy Ann's house, Miss Sadie
was sitting helpless and hopeless before her—the

whole scene was vivid and complete. She paused; her arm, which had been outstretched and rigid for an instant, slowly fell to her side, and—the illusion was gone; but while it lasted, it was as real as any sudden and extraordinary experience can be.

Aunt Minervy Ann resumed her seat, with a chuckle, apparently ashamed that she had been betrayed into such a display of energy and emotion, saying, " Yessum, she sho' went."

" I don't wonder at it," remarked the lady of the house, with a long-drawn sigh of relief.

Aunt Minervy Ann laughed again, rather sheepishly, and then, after rubbing her hands together, took up the thread of the narrative, this time directing her words to me: " All de way ter de house, suh, she ain't say two words. She had holt er my han', but she ain't walk like she uz weak. She went along ez peart ez I did. When we got dar, some er de niggers wuz out in de flower gyarden an' out in de big grove callin' 'er; an' dey call so loud dat I hatter put um down. ' Hush up!' I say, ' an' go on 'bout yo' business! Can't yo' Miss Sadie take a walk widout a whole passel er you niggers a-hollerin' yo' heads off?' One un um make answer, ' Miss Fanny huntin' fer 'er.' She sorter grip my han' at dat,

but I say, ' She de one you wanter see—her an'
Gabe Towers.'

"We went up on de po'ch, an' dar wuz Miss
Fanny an' likewise Marse Gabe. I know'd what
dey wanted; dey wanted ter talk wid 'er 'bout Marse
Jesse. She clum de steps fus' an' I clum atter
her. She cotch er 'breff hard when she fus' hit de
steps, an' den it come over me like a flash how
deep an' big her trouble wuz, an' I tell you right
now, ef dat had 'a' been Miss Vallie gwine up dar,
I b'lieve I'd 'a' flew at ol' Gab Towers an' to' 'im
lim' fum lim' 'fo' anybody could 'a' pull me off.
Hit's de trufe! You may laugh, but I sho' would
'a' done it. I had it in me. Miss Fanny seed
sump'n wuz wrong, de minnit de light fell on de gal's
face. She say, ' Why, Sadie, darlin', what de matter wid you? '—des so—an' made ez ef ter put 'er
arms 'roun 'er; but Miss Sadie swunk back. Miss
Fanny sorter swell up. She say, ' Oh, ef I've
hurt yo' feelin's ter-day—*ter-day* uv all de days
—please, please fergi' me! ' Well, suh, I dunner
whar all dis gwine ter lead ter, an' I put in,
' She des wanter have a talk wid you an' Marse
Gabe, Miss Fanny; an' ef ter-day is one er de
days her feelin's oughtn'ter be hurted, take keer
dat you don't do it. Kyar 'er in de parler dar, Miss

62

Fanny.' I 'speck you'll think I wuz takin' a mighty heap on myse'f, fer a nigger 'oman," remarked Aunt Minervy Ann, smoothing the wrinkles out of her lap, " but I wuz des ez much at home in dat house ez I wuz in my own, an' des ez free wid um ez I wuz wid my own folks. Miss Fanny look skeer'd, an' Marse Gabe foller'd atter, rubbin' a little mole he had on de top er his head. When he wus worried er aggervated, he allers rub dat mole.

" Well, suh, dey went in, dey did, an' I shot de do' an' tuck up my stan' close by, ready fer to go in when Miss Sadie call me. I had myse'f keyed up ter de p'int whar I'd 'a' tol' Marse Gabe sump'n 'bout his own fambly connection; you know dey ain't nobody but what got i'on rust on some er der cloze. But dey stayed in dar an' stayed, twel I 'gun ter git oneasy. All kinder quare idees run th'oo my head. Atter while some un pull de do' open, an' hol' it dat away, an' I hear Marse Gabe say, wid a trimble an' ketch in his th'oat, ' Don't talk so, chil'. Ef you done wrong, you ain't hurt nobody but yo'se'f, an' it oughtn'ter hurt you. You been a mighty big blessin' ter me, an' ter Fanny here, an' I wouldn't 'a' missed knowin' you, not fer nothin'. Wid dat, he come out cle'rin up his th'oat an' blowin' his nose twel it soun' like a dinner-horn. His eye fell on me, an' he 'low, ' Look like you er allers on han' when dey's trouble.' I made answer, ' Well, Marse Gabe, dey might be wusser ones 'roun' dan me.' He look at me right hard an' say, ' Dey ain't no better, Minervy Ann.' Well, suh, little mo' an' I'd 'a' broke down, it come so sudden. I had ter gulp hard an' quick, I tell you. He say, ' Minervy Ann, go back dar an' tell de house-gal ter wake up de carriage-driver ef he's 'sleep, an' tell 'im to go meet Jesse at de train. An' he mus' tell Jesse dat we'd 'a' all come, but his ma ain't feelin' so well.' I say, ' I'll go wake 'im up myse'f, suh.' I look in de parler an' say, ' Miss Sadie, does you need me right now?' She 'low, ' No, not right now; I'll stay twel—twel Mr. Towers come.' Miss Fanny wuz settin' dar holdin' Miss Sadie's han'.

" I'll never tell you how dey patcht it up in dar, but I made a long guess. Fus' an' fo'mus', dey wuz right down fon' er Miss Sadie, an' den ef she run off time Marse Jesse put his foot in de town dey'd be a big scandal; an' so dey fix it up dat ef she wuz bleeze ter go, 'twuz better to go a mont' er two atter Marse Jesse come back. Folks may like you mighty well, but dey allers got one eye on der own consarns. Dat de way I put it down.

" Well, suh, de wuss job wuz lef' fer de las', 'kaze

dar wuz Marse Jesse. Sump'n tol' me dat he oughter know what been gwine on 'fo' he got in de house, 'kaze den he won't be aggervated inter sayin' an' doin' sump'n he oughtn'ter. So when de carriage wuz ready, I got in an' went down ter de depot; an' when Marse Jesse got off de train, I wuz de fus' one he laid eyes on. I'd 'a' never know'd 'im in de worl', but he know'd me. He holler out, 'Ef dar ain't Aunt Minervy Ann! Bless yo' ol' soul! how you come on anyhow?' He come mighty nigh huggin' me, he wuz so glad ter see me. He wuz big ez a skinned hoss an' strong ez a mule. He say, ' Ef I had you in my min' once, Aunt Minervy Ann, I had you in dar ten thousan' times.'

" Whiles de carriage rollin' 'long an' grindin' de san' I try ter gi' 'im a kinder inkling er what been gwine on, but 'twuz all a joke wid 'im. I wuz fear'd I mought go at 'im de wrong way, but I can't do no better. I say, ' Marse Jesse, yo' wife been waitin' here fer you a long time.' He laugh an' 'low, ' Oh, yes! did she bring de childun?' I say, ' Shucks, Marse Jesse! Dey's a lady in deep trouble at Marse Gabe's house, an' I don't want you ter go dar jokin'. She's a monst'us fine lady, too.' Dis kinder steady 'im, an' he say, ' All right, Aunt Minervy Ann; I'll behave myse'f des like a Sunday-school scholar. I won't say bad words an' I won't talk loud.' He had his fiddle-case in his lap, an' hè drummed on it like he keepin' time ter some chune in his min'.

"Well, suh, we got dar in de due time, an' 'twuz a great meetin' 'twixt Marse Jesse an' his folks. Dey des swarmed on 'im, ez you may say, an' while dis gwine on, I went in de parler whar Miss Sadie wuz. She wuz pale, tooby sha', but she had done firm'd 'erse'f. She wuz standin' by de fier-place, lookin' down, but she lookt up when she hear de do' open, an' den she say, ' I'm mighty glad it's you, Aunt Minervy Ann; I want you ter stay in here.' I 'low, ' I'll stay, honey, ef you say stay.' Den she tuck 'er stand by me an' cotch holt er my arm wid bofe 'er han's an' kinder leant ag'in me.

"Bimeby, here come Marse Jesse. Trouble wuz in his eye when he open de do', but when he saw de gal, his face lit up des like when you strike a match in a closet. He say, ' Why, Miss Sadie! You dunner how glad I is ter see you. I been huntin' all over de country fer you.' He make ez ef ter shake han's, but she draw'd back. Dis cut 'im. He say: ' What de matter? Who you in mournin' fer?' She 'low, ' Fer myse'f.' Wid dat she wuz gwine on ter tel 'im 'bout what she had done, but he wouldn't have it dat way. He say, ' When I come back ter

life, atter I wuz drownded, I 'gun ter hunt fer you
des ez soon's I got out'n de hospittle. I wuz huntin'
fer you ter tell you dat I love you. I'd 'a' tol' you
dat den, an' I tell you dat now.' She grip my arm
mighty hard at dat. Marse Jesse went on mightly.
He tell 'er dat she ain't done nobody no harm, dat
she wuz welcome ter his name ef he'd 'a' been dead,
an' mo' welcome now dat he wuz livin'. She try ter
put in a word here an' dar, but he won't have it.
Stan'in' up dar he wuz ol' Gabe Towers over ag'in;
'twuz de fus' time I know'd he faver'd 'im.

" He tol' 'er 'bout how he wrenched a do' off'n
one er de rooms in de boat, an' how he floated on dat
twel he got so col' an' num' dat he can't hol' on no
longer, an' how he turn loose an' don't know nothin'
twel he wake up in some yuther town; an' how,
atter he git well, he had de plooisy an' lay dar a
mont' er two, an' den he 'gun ter hunt fer her. He
went 'way up dar ter Hampsher whar she come fum,
but she ain't dar, an' den he come home; an' won't
she be good 'nuff ter set down an' listen at 'im?

" Well, suh, dey wuz mo' in Marse Jesse dan I
had any idee. He wuz a rank talker, sho'. I see 'er
face warmin' up, an' I say, ' Miss Sadie, I 'speck I
better be gwine.' Marse Jesse say, ' You ain't in
my way, Aunt Minervy Ann; I done foun' my

sweetheart, an' I ain't gwine ter lose 'er no mo', you kin des bet on dat.' She ain't say nothin' an' I know'd purty well dat eve'ything wuz all skew vee."

"I hope they married," remarked the lady of the house, after waiting a moment for Aunt Minervy Ann to resume. There was just a shade of suspicion in her tone.

"Oh, dey married, all right 'nuff," said Aunt Minervy Ann, laughing.

"Didn't it create a good deal of talk?" the lady asked, suspicion still in her voice.

"Talk? No, ma'm! De man what dey git de license fum wuz Miss Fanny's br'er, Gus Feather-stone, an' de man what married um wuz Marse Gabe's bro'er, John Towers. Dey wa'n't nobody ter do no talkin'. De nex' mornin' me an' Miss Sadie an' Marse Jesse got in de carriage an' drove out ter John Towers's place whar he runnin' a church, an' 'twuz all done an' over wid mos' quick ez a nigger kin swaller a dram."

"What do you think of it?" I asked the lady of the house.

"Why, it is almost like a story in a book."

"Does dey put dat kinder doin's in books?" asked Aunt Minervy Ann, with some solicitude.

"Certainly," replied the lady.

" Wid all de turmile, an' trouble, an' tribulation —an' all de worry an' aggervation? Well, Hamp wanted me ter l'arn how ter read, but I thank my stars dat I can't read no books. Dey's 'nuff er all dat right whar we live at widout huntin' it up in books."

After this just observation, it was time to put out the lights.

III

HOW AUNT MINERVY ANN RAN AWAY AND RAN BACK AGAIN

In the matter of attending the fair at Halcyondale, Aunt Minervy Ann's hospitable wishes jumped with my own desires, and it was not difficult to give her a hard and fast promise in the matter; nor did it take the edge off my desires to entertain a suspicion, verified long afterward, that Aunt Minervy Ann's anxiety was based on a hope, expressed by Major Perdue, that the fair would be properly handled in the Atlanta papers.

The directors of the fair were represented at the little railway station, at Halcyondale, by a committee, and into the hands of this committee fell every man, woman, and child that stepped from the passing trains. It mattered little what the business of these incoming travellers was; whether they came to visit the fair or to attend to their own private affairs. They were seized, bag and baggage, by the committee and borne triumphantly to the hotel, or to a boarding-place, or to some private house. The members of the committee had a duty to perform, and they performed it with an energy and a thoroughness that was amazing if not altogether satisfactory. As I remember, this vigorous body was called the Committee on Public Comfort, and most heroically did it live up to its name and its duties.

These things I learned by observation and not by experience, for before the train on which I was a passenger had cleared the suburbs of Atlanta, I caught a glimpse of Major Tumlin Perdue, who had long been a prominent citizen of Halcyondale. He had changed but little during the ten years. His hair was whiter, and he was a trifle thinner, but his complexion was still rosy and his manners as buoyant as ever. I doubted whether he would know me again, though he had been very friendly with me in the old days, seeming to know by instinct just when and how to drop a word of encouragement and appreciation, and so I forbore to renew the acquaintance. The Major could be boisterous enough in those times when in the humor, but when at his best he had more ways like those of a woman (and a noble and tender-hearted woman at that) than any man I had ever known. He had a woman's tact, intuition, and sympathy; and these quali-

71

ties were so exquisitely developed in him that they lifted him high in the estimation of a young man who was living away from his mother, and who was somewhat lonely on that account.

Presently, the Major came along the aisle for a drink of water. As he was in the act of drinking, his eyes met mine, and he recognized me instantly. He swallowed the water with a gulp.

" Why, bless my soul! " he exclaimed, greeting me with the simple cordiality that springs from an affectionate nature. " Why, I wouldn't take ten dollars for this! I was thinking about you this very day. Don't you remember the night we went out to ku-klux the Ku-klux, and the chap that mighty nigh broke his neck running into a wire clothes-line? I saw him to-day. He would hardly speak to me," the Major went on, laughing heartily. " He's never got over that night's business. I thought about you, and I started to hunt you up; but you know how it is in Atlanta. Folks ain't got time to eat, much less to tell you where anybody lives. A man that's too busy is bound to worry, and worry will kill him every bit and grain as quick as John Barleycorn. Business is bound to be the ruin of this country, and if you don't live to see it, your children will."

Thus the Major talked, blending wisdom with

72

The Committee of Public Comfort.

impracticable ideas in the most delightful way. He
seemed to be highly pleased when he found that I
was to spend a week at Halcyondale, attending the
fair and renewing old friendships.

" Then you belong to me! " he exclaimed. " It's
no use," he went on, shaking his head when I
would have protested against imposing on his good-
nature; " you needn't say a word. The tavern is
stuffed full of people, and even if it wasn't, you'd
go to my house. If you ain't been ruined by living
in Atlanta, it'll seem like home to you. Dang it all!
I'll *make* it seem like home to you anyhow."

Now, the affectation of hospitality is one of the
commonest hypocrisies in life, and, to a thoughtful
man, one of the most sinister; but the Major's hospitality was genuine. It was brought over from the
times before the war, and had stood the test of age
and long usage, and, most trying of all, the test of
poverty. " If you were welcome when I was well
off, how much more welcome you'll be now that I
am poor! " This was not said by the Major, but by
one of his contemporaries. The phrase fitted a
whole generation of noble men and women, and I
thank Heaven that it was true at one time even if it
is not true now.

When the train, with much clinking and clank-

ing and hissing, came to a standstill at Halcyondale,
the Major hustled me off on the side opposite the
station, and so I escaped the ordeal of resisting the
efforts of the Committee on Public Comfort to con-
vey me to a lodging not of my own selection. The
Major's buggy was in waiting, with a negro driver,
who got out to make room for me. He bowed very
politely, calling me by name.

" You remember Hamp, I reckon," said the Major. " He was a member of the Legislature when
you lived here."

Certainly I remembered Hamp, who was Aunt
Minervy Ann's husband. I inquired about her, and
Hamp, who had swung up to the trunk-rack as
the buggy moved off, replied that she was at home
and as well as she could be.

" Yes," said the Major, " she's at my house. You
may *see* somebody else besides Minervy Ann, but
you won't *hear* anybody else. She owns the whole
place and the people on it. I had a Boston man to
dinner some time ago, one of Conant's friends—
you remember Paul Conant, don't you?—and I
stirred Minervy Ann up just to see what the man
would say. We had a terrible quarrel, and the man
never did know it was all in fun. He said they
never would have such a lack of discipline among

the servants in Boston. I told him I would give him any reasonable amount if he would go out and discipline Minervy Ann, just to show me how it was done. It would have been better than a circus. You heard her, didn't you, Hamp?"

Hamp chuckled good-naturedly. " Yasser, I did, an' it make col' chills run over me ter hear how Minervy Ann went on. She cert'n'y did try herse'f dat day."

The Major smiled a little proudly as I thought, slapped the horse—a bob-tailed black—with the left rein, and we went skimming along the level, sandy street at a three-minute gait. In a short while we were at the Major's house, where I received a warm welcome from his daughter, whom I had known when she was a school-girl. She was now Mrs. Paul Conant, and even more beautiful as a matron than she had been as a girl. I had also known her husband, who had begun his business career in the town a year or two before I left, and even at that time he was one of the most prominent and promising young business men in the town.

He had served in the army the last year of the war, and the service did him a world of good, physically and mentally. His faculties were broadened and enlarged. Contact with all sorts and conditions of men gave him ample knowledge of his kind, and yet he kept in touch with the finer issues of life. He was ripened and not hardened.

The surrender had no such crushing effects on him as it had on older men. It left him youth, and where youth is there must be hope and energy. He returned home, remained a few weeks, sold a couple of horses he had picked up in the track of Sherman's army, and then went into the office of a cotton factor in Savannah, giving his services for the knowledge and experience he desired to gain. In a very short time he learned all the secrets of sampling and grading the great staple. He might have remained in the office at a salary, for his aptness had made him useful, but he preferred to return to Halcyondale, where he engaged in buying cotton on his own account. There was just enough risk in this to stimulate his energies, and not enough to lead to serious speculation.

To this business he added others as his capital grew, and he was soon the most prosperous man in the town. He had formed the stock company under whose auspices the county fair was held, and was president of the board of directors.

Aunt Minervy Ann was very much in evidence, for she acted as cook, nurse, and house-girl. The

Buying cotton on his own account.

first glimpse I had of her, she had a bucket of water in her right hand and Conant's baby—a bouncing boy—on her left arm. Just then Major Perdue hustled me off to my room, thus postponing, as I thought, the greeting I had for Aunt Minervy Ann. But presently I heard her coming upstairs talking to herself.

"Ef dey gwine ter have folks puttin' up wid um, dey better tell me in de due time, so I can fix up fer um. Dey ain't been no fresh water in deze rooms sence dat baby wuz born'd."

She went on to the end of the hall and looked in each of the rooms. Then, with an exclamation I failed to catch, she knocked at my door, which was promptly opened. As she saw me a broad smile flashed over her good-natured face.

"I 'low'd 'twuz you," she said, "an' I'm mighty glad you come." She started to pour the water from can to pitcher, when suddenly she stayed her hand. With the exclamation, "Well, ef dis don't bang my time!" she went to the head of the stairs and cried out: "Miss Vallie! Miss Vallie! you don't want no town folks stuck in dish yer back room, does you?"

"Why, certainly not!" cried the lady. "What could father have been thinking of?"

"Shoo! he like all de men folks," responded Aunt Minervy Ann.

With that she seized my valise with one hand, and, carrying the can of water in the other, escorted me to one of the front rooms. It was an improvement on the back room only because it had more windows to admit the air and light. I put in a word for the Major, which I hoped would be carried to the ears of the daughter.

"The Major gave me that room because he wanted to treat me as if I were one of the home folks. Now you've brought me here, and I'll feel as uncomfortable as if I were company, sure enough."

"Dey's sump'n in dat, I 'speck," replied Aunt Minervy Ann, laughing; "but, lawsy, massy! you done been in dis house too much ter talk dat-a-way. When kin folks come home, we allus gin um de bes' dey is fer de fus' week er so. Atter dat dey kin rustle 'roun' fer deyse'f."

It is hardly necessary to say that Aunt Minervy Ann took very good care that I should want for none of those little attentions that sharpen the appreciation of a guest; and, in her case, obtrusiveness was not a fault, for her intentions shone clearly and unmistakably through it all.

78

" Miss Vallie ! "

Major Perdue had the art of entertainment at his fingers' ends, which, though it is very simple, not one man in a hundred learns. It is the knack of leaving the guest to his own devices without seeming to do so. Most fortunate in his gifts is the host who knows how to temper his attentions!

In his efforts to get the fair under way, Paul Conant found it impossible to come to dinner, but sent his apologies.

" You'll think it is a mighty small concern when you see it," said the Major, " but it takes all that Paul can do to keep it from getting into a tangle. He has to be here, there, and everywhere, and there hasn't been a minute for a week or more but what forty people were hollering at him at once, and forty more pulling and hauling him about. If he wasn't a steam-engine, he couldn't hold out half an hour."

" Well, he'll soon straighten matters out," said I, " and then they'll stay so."

" That's so," remarked the Major; " but when that's done, he'll have to rush around from post to pillar to keep 'em straight."

" Did he seem to be greatly worried? " Valentine asked.

" No-o-o-o," replied the Major, slowly and hesitatingly, " but I'm afear'd his shoulder has begun

79

to trouble him again." He leaned back in his chair and looked at the ceiling, apparently lost in thought.

" Why should you think that, father? "

" Once or twice, whilst he was rustling about I saw him fling his hand to his shoulder and hold it there, and I'm mightily afear'd it's hurting him." The Major drew a deep sigh as he spoke, and silence fell on all. It was brief, but it was long enough for one to know that an unpleasant subject had been touched on—that there was something more behind it all than a pain in Conant's shoulder. Aunt Minervy Ann, who was equal to every emergency, created a diversion with the baby, and the Major soon pulled himself together.

Paul Conant came home to supper, and in the sitting-room, before the meal was announced, I observed that the Major was as solicitous about him as a mother is of her baby. His eyes were constantly on his son-in-law, and if the latter showed any sign of worry, or frowned as if in pain, a shadow would pass over the Major's genial face.

This intense solicitude was something out of the usual order, and I wondered what was behind it. But the next day it was forgotten, nor was it remembered until Aunt Minervy Ann reminded me of it. I had been faithful in my attendance on the fair,

"I saw him fling his hand to his shoulder and hold it there."

had listened patiently to the speeches, and had then tried to refresh my benumbed faculties with such fare as could be found on the grounds—barbecue, pickles, and ginger-cakes. But the occasion had been too much for me, and so, about two o'clock in the afternoon, I decided to return to my quarters at Major Perdue's home and rest my weary limbs. The very thought of the quiet and cool house was refreshing, and so, without waiting for a conveyance, I set out on foot, going through the woods in preference to the public highway, thereby cutting the distance short by nearly a mile.

A great many others had taken advantage of the short-cut through the woods, so that I had no lack of company. Among them I noticed Aunt Minervy and her husband, Hamp, the latter carrying the Conant baby, which, having had enough of the pomps and vanities of this life for the time being, was now fast asleep. I soon came up with the trio, and we went along home together.

"You toughed it out mighty well, suh," remarked Aunt Minervy Ann, after some talk about the various attractions of the fair. "Up dar in Atlanty deze kinder doin's would be laughed at, I 'speck, but hit's de bes' we-all kin do. Me an' Miss Vallie had some truck

81

dar, speshually dat ar grape jelly on de right han' side. Ef dat jelly don't git de blue ribbon er sump'n better, hit'll be bakaze dem ar jedgment men ain't got no sense—I don't keer who dey is. Ain't you see dat ar quilt hangin' up dar wid a pattern in it like a well-whorl, only de middle er de whorl was shape like de mornin' star? Dat ar quilt is older dan what you is, suh—lots older. Me an' Mistiss made dat quilt long 'fo' Miss Vallie wuz born, an' dish yer baby'll tell you she ain't no chicken. Ef dey's any purtier quilt on dat hill dey had it hid ter-day; dey ain't brung it out whar folks kin look at it. I dunno much, but I knows dat much."

We reached the house after awhile, and I lost no time in stretching myself out on a lounge that sat invitingly in the hall behind the stairway. It was not the coolest place in the world; but, really, when one is fagged out, it is unnecessary to try to find all the comforts of life in one spot. Sleep fell on me unawares, and when I awoke, Aunt Minervy Ann was sitting near the head of the lounge fanning me. Such courtesy was surprising, as well as pleasing, but I chid her for taking so much trouble, for I had slept nearly two hours. But she made light of it, saying she had nothing else to do, the baby being in his cradle and sleeping like a log.

"Dat ar grape jelly on de right han' side."

Then, to enjoy a smoke, I drew a rocking-chair into the back porch, and proceeded to fill my pipe with what I regarded as a very good brand of to-bacco, offering some to Aunt Minervy Ann. She soon found her pipe—clay bowl and reed stem—cleaned it out carefully and filled it from my pouch.

"It look mighty pale, suh," she remarked. "I 'speck dey steam it 'fo' dey mash it up." She seated herself on the top step, lit her pipe, took a few whiffs, and then shook her head. " 'Tain't nigh rank 'nuff for me, suh. Hit tas'e like you er dreamin' 'bout smokin' an' know all de time 'tain't nothin' but a dream." She knocked the tobacco out, and then re-filled the pipe with the crumbs and cutting from the end of a plug. This she smoked with an air of su-preme satisfaction.

"I 'speck you got de idee dat I better be seein' 'bout supper, stidder settin' up here lookin' biggity. But 'tain't no use, suh. Marse Tumlin and Miss Vallie never is ter come home dis day less'n dey bring Marse Paul wid um. I done hear um sesso. An' I know mighty well, deyer gwine ter come back late, bekaze Paul Conant's one er dem kinder folks what go twel dey can't go, an' when dey git down dey make motions like dey gwine. Dey puts me in mind uv a lizard's tail, suh. Knock it off, an' it'll hop 'bout an' work an' wiggle plum twel de sun go down."

I suggested that the illustration was somewhat inapt (though not in those words), for the reason that Paul Conant's energy was not expended blindly. But I found that Aunt Minervy knew what she was saying.

" I ain't talkin' 'bout his own business, suh, bekaze dey ain't nobody beat 'im at dat. No, suh; I'm talkin' 'bout dem ar doin's out dar at de fair groun's. He's a-workin' at dat lots harder dan he has ter work fer hisse'f. Maybe you tuck notice uv de way dem yuther folks done out dar, suh. Dey stood 'round wid dey mouf open, an' de ribbon pinned on der coats, an' when sump'n had ter be done, dey'd call out fer Conant. It 'uz ' Conant! ' here an' ' Conant! ' dar, an' ef Conant wuz out er hearin' de whole shebang had ter stop right still an' wait twel Conant kin be dragged up. I watched um p'intedly, suh, an' it's des like I tell you."

Aunt Minervy Ann's characterization of the directors was so acute and so unexpected that I laughed—not at what she said, but at the vivid picture of a lot of helpless men standing about, full of dignity, and yet waiting for young Conant to tell them what to do.

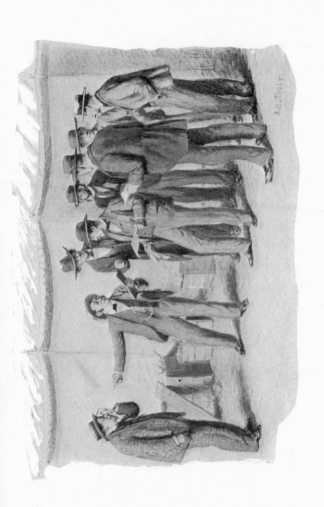

"'Conant!' here and 'Conant!' dar,"

"You may laugh, suh," Aunt Minervy Ann went on with a little frown, "but I'm tellin' you de Lord's trufe. I kep' my eyes on um, an' 'twuz dat-a-way fum soon dis mornin' 'twel I got mad an' come home. You kin ax Hamp, suh, an' he'll tell you de same. I reckon you heer'd Marse Tumlin las' night at de table ax Marse Paul ef his shoulder hurted 'im. I know you did, suh, bekaze I tuck notice how you looked, an' I tried ter shake de baby up so he'd cry, but dat wuz one er de times, suh, when he wouldn't be shuck up. Any udder time dat chil' would er laid back an' blated twel you'd hafter put yo' fingers in yo' years. I wuz mad wid 'im, suh, but I wuz bleedz ter laugh. Chillun mighty funny. When you don't want um ter cry, dey'll holler der heads off, an' when you want um ter cry, dey'll laugh in yo' face. I bet you dey's a blue place on dat baby's arm whar I pinched 'im, but he didn't no mo' min' it dan nothin'."

"Well," said I, "there was something peculiar in the way all of you looked and acted when the Major asked about Mr. Conant's shoulder. It was a very simple question."

"Ah, Lord!" exclaimed Aunt Minervy Ann, raising her right hand on high, "dey better ax 'bout dat shoulder. Yesser! ev'y day an' ev'y night, an' in betwixt times."

"Is Mr. Conant troubled with rheumatism?" I inquired.

"Rheumatiz! bless yo' soul, honey! Ef 'twuz rheumatiz dey wouldn't be no Paul Conant 'round dis house, ner no Conant baby."

Here is something decidedly interesting, I thought, but held my peace, knowing that whatever it was would be more quickly disclosed if there were any disclosure to make.

"Ain't you never hear 'bout it, suh? Well dat bangs me! An' you right up dar in Atlanty, too! No, suh; you must er been in Savanny, bekaze 'twuz de town talk in Atlanty. Anyhow, whar-somever you wuz er might er been, dey ain't no rheumatiz de matter wid Marse Paul Conant's shoulder-blade. I know dat much, an' I know it mighty well, bekaze I wuz right here in dis house, an' nowhars else 'cep'n 'roun' de lot an' up town an' back.

"Well, den, suh, ef you ain't never hear 'bout dat, I most know you ain't never hear tell er how I run'd off, and how I run'd back, bekaze nobody ain't never talk 'bout dat—leas'ways, not as I knows un."

I declared to Aunt Minervy Ann that I never heard a whisper of it. She leaned back against the railing of the steps and drew a long whiff from her pipe.

" 'Tain't no use ter tell you, suh, how times wuz right atter de war. You wuz right in um, an' ef you don't know, it's bekaze you didn't look 'roun' an' see um. I hear um say, suh, dat niggers wuz po' when dey come free. Dey wuz, suh; dey wuz rank pizen po'; but dey never wuz in dis worl' a nigger ez po' ez some er our white folks wuz. You may shake yo' haid, suh, but I'm givin' you de straight gov'nment trufe. Niggers is use ter bein' po', an' dey never wuz dat po' dat dey can't scuffle 'roun' an' make out somehow. Dey er been po' so long dey er usen ter it. But white folks what been rich! I hope de Lord'll call me home 'fo' I see again what I done saw in dem days. I know in reason, suh, dat I seed mo' er de trouble dan what you did, kaze you couldn't go in at de back gates like me; an' what trouble folks does have dey allers keep it somers betwix' de bedroom an' de back gate.

" De Perdues wa'n't no wuss off dan nobody else. Marse Tumlin had dish yer house an' lot, an' de plantation, an' some lan' way off yander. But all de hosses an' mules an' cattle been tuck off, an' de

87

niggers all gone. Ef he'd er stayed on de plantation, de niggers would 'a' been dar yit, but stay he
wouldn't, an' stay he didn't, an' so dar he wuz.

"Do sump'n? What he gwine do? Fo' de big
turmoil he done some lawin' an' a heap er farmin'.
Leas'ways my ol' Mistiss done de farmin', an' Marse
Tumlin, he done de lawin'. He had 'im a office here
in town, an' on set days he'd come in an' look arter
de cases what he had. But how anybody gwine ter
do any lawin' dat-a-way? Marse Tumlin ain't keerin' whedder he git one case er none. He ain't
bleedze ter do no lawin'. An' den 'pon top
er dat he went off whar dey battlin', an' dar he
stayed, an' when he come back, look like de kinder
lawin' what he use ter do done gone outer fashion.
Ef he hadn't er been holp out, suh, I dunner what'd
'a' come un 'im. An' 'twa'n't only Marse Tumlin.
Dey wuz a whole passel un um, too young ter die
an' too ol' ter win money in dem kinder times. Ef
you ain't ol' 'nuff ter 'member dem times, suh, you
kin thank de Lord, kaze dey sho did look like tetotal
ruination.

"Now, you know yo'se'f, suh, dat you can't eat
a house an' lot an' live dar too; an' you can't eat lan'
des dry so less'n you got a mighty appetite fer dirt.
Whyn't he sell de lan'? You oughter be de las' one

ter ax me dat, suh. Who gwine buy it? Dem what
ain't got lan' ain't had no money, an' dem what had
money sholy lived a mighty long ways fum here.
Day in an' day out, suh, I wuz de wuss pester'd
nigger you ever laid eyes on. I ain't know what
ter do.

" An' den 'pon top er dat, dar wuz Hamp, my ol'
man. When freedom come out, he tuck de notion
dat we better go off some'rs an' change de name
what we got so dey can't put us back in slave'y.
Night an' day it fair rankle in his min', an' he kep'
groanin' an' growlin' 'bout it twel I got stirred up.
I oughtn't ter tell it, suh, but hit's de Lord's trufe.
I got mad, I did, an' I tol' Hamp I'd go. An' den
I wa'n't doin' no good stayin' here. 'Twuz des
one mo' mouf ter feed, an' mo' dan one, countin'
Hamp. So, bimeby, one day, when I wuz sorter
fretted, I tol' Hamp ter go on out dar in de country, whar his daddy live at, an' I'd meet 'im dar
'fo' night.

" When de time come, I went in de house an'
hunt fer Miss Vallie. She 'uz settin' in de parlor
by de winder, but behime de curtain like, so nobody
can't see 'er. She 'uz settin' dar wid 'er han's
crossed on 'er lap, an' she look so little, an' pale, an'
weak, dat I come mighty nigh gwine right back in

89

de kitchen. But she seed me too quick. Den I up'n tell 'er dat I'm gwine out in de country, ter whar Hamp daddy live at. She look at me right hard an' say, ' When you comin' back, Aunt Minervy Ann?' I 'low, ' I'm comin' back des ez soon ez I kin make my 'rangements, honey.' She say, ' Well, I hope you'll have a good time while you er gone.' I 'low, ' Thanky, ma'm.' Wid dat I went an' got my bundle an' put opt fum dar—an' I ain't look back nudder, bekaze I had a mighty weakness in de knees, an' a mighty risin' in my th'oat.

" I went on down de road, an' ef anybody had so much ez said *boo* ter me, I'd 'a' turned right 'roun' an' gone back home. I went on, I did, twel I come ter de mile branch. I see somebody crossin' on de log, an' when I come up wid um, who should it 'a' been but Marse Tumlin. An' he had *one chicken!* He had been out ter de plantation—sev'm mile ef its fifty yards—an' here he wuz comin' back wid one chicken— an' him a walkin', him dat use ter ride 'roun' in his carriage! Walkin' an' totin' one little chicken! Man, suh! I don't never want ter feel again like I felt den. Whedder 'twuz de chicken, er what, I never did see Marse Tumlin Perdue look ez 'ol' an' ez weasly ez he did den. He look at me an' sorter laugh like I done cotch 'im doin' sump'n

"Drapt down on de groun' dar an' holler an' cry."

he ain't got no business ter do. But dey wa'n't no laugh in me; no, suh, not by a jugful.

"He say, 'Hello, Minervy Ann! whar *you* gwine?' I 'low, I did, 'I'm des gwine out yander whar Hamp kinnery live at.'

"He sorter pull his goatee, an' look down at de dus' on his shoes—an' dey wuz fair kiver'd wid it—an' den he say, 'Well, Minervy Ann, I wish you mighty well. You sho is done a mighty good part by me an' mine. Ef yo' Miss Mary wuz 'live she'd know what ter say—I don't, 'cep' dis'—he straighten up an' stretch out his han'—''cep' dis: whenever you want ter come back home, you'll fin' de do' open. Ef you come at night, des knock. We'll know yo' knock.'

"You ain't never seed no fool nigger 'oman cut up, is you? Well, ef you does see one, suh, I hope ter goodness 'twon't be me! Marse Tumlin ain't no mo'n got de words out'n his mouf, suh, 'fo' I tuck de bundle what I had in my han', an' flung it fur ez I could send it.

"Marse Tumlin look at me hard, an' den he say, 'Dam ef I don't b'lieve youer crazy!' Time he say it, I 'low, '*I don't keer er dam ef I is!*'

"Yasser! I say it sho, an' den I drapt down on de groun' dar an' holler an' cry like somebody wuz

91

beatin' de life out'n me. Marse Tumlin stood dar
pullin' at his goatee all dat time, an' bimeby I got
up. I wa'n't feelin' much better, but I done had my
cry an' dat's sump'n. I got up, I did, an' start back
de way I come.

" Marse Tumlin say, ' Whar you gwine, Minervy
Ann? I 'low, ' I'm gwine back home—dat's whar
I'm gwine!' He say, ' Pick up yo' bundle.' Wid
dat I turn 'roun' on him an' 'low, ' I ain't gwine ter
do it! Ef it hadn't er been fer dat ar muslin dress
in dar, what Miss Vallie make over an' gi' me, I'd
been at home right dis minute.'

" He 'low, ' What dat got ter do wid it, Minervy
Ann?' I make answer, ' Bekaze ol' Satan make me
want ter put it on an' sho' off 'fo' dem country niggers out dar whar Hamp's folks live at.' Wid dat
I start back home, but Marse Tumlin holler at me—
' Minervy Ann, take dis chicken.' I tuck it, I did,
an' made off up de road. Bimeby I sorter flung my
eye 'roun', an', bless gracious! dar wuz Marse Tumlin comin' 'long totin' my bundle. Well, suh, it
flewed all over me like fier. I got so mad wid myse'f dat I could 'a' bit a piece out'n my own flesh.

" I waited in de road twel he come up, an' den I
snatched de bundle out er his han'. I 'low, ' I ain't
gwine ter have you totin' none er my bundles in de

public road—no, ner no chickens, needer.' He say,
' Well, don't fling it 'way, Minervy Ann. De time
may come when yo' Miss Vallie'll need dat ar muslin dress.'

" When we got back home I went in de kitchen,
an' fix ter clean an' kill de chicken. I 'speck Marse
Tumlin must 'a' tol' Miss Vallie 'bout it, bekaze
'twan't long 'fo' I hear her runnin' 'long de plank
walk ter de kitchen. She whipt in de do' she did,
an' grab me an' cry like I done riz fum de dead.
Well, suh, niggers ain't got no sense, you kin take
um de world over. No sooner is Miss Vallie start
ter cry dan I chuned up, an' dar we had it.

" 'Bout dat time, Marse Tumlin, he come out—
men folks is allers gwine some'rs dey got no business. He 'low, ' What you'all blubberin' 'bout?'
I make answer, ' We er cryin' over dese two chickens.' He ax, ' What two chickens?' I 'low, ' I'm
cryin' over dis un, kaze it's so little, an' Miss Vallie
cryin' over de one what you ain't brung. He say,
' Well, I be dang!' an' wid dat he went back in de
house.

" An' den, atter supper, such ez 'twuz, here come
Hamp, an' he say he come ter lay de law down. I
'speck I like my ol' man 'bout ez good ez any udder
'oman what's lawfully married, but ef I didn't put a

93

flea in Hamp year dat night you may shoot me dead. Ef he'd 'a' waited a day er two, hit might er been diffunt; but, manlike, he had ter come at de wrong time, an' he ain't open his mouf 'fo' I wuz fightin' mad. Ol' Miss allers use ter tell me I wuz a bad nigger when I got my dander up, but I never did look at myse'f dat-a-way twel dat night.

"Well, Hamp he come an' stood in de do', but I ain't say nothin'. Den he come in de kitchen, an' stan' 'roun', but still I ain't say nothin'. Den he sot down next de chimbley, but all dat time I ain't say nothin'. He look right pitiful, suh, an' ef I hadn't been mad, I'd 'a' been sorry fer 'im. But I ain't say nothin'.

"Bimeby, he 'low, ' 'Nervy '—he allers call me 'Nervy—' 'Nervy, whyn't you go whar you say you gwine?' I flung myse'f 'roun' at 'im an' say, ' Bekaze I ain't choosen ter go—dar you got it!' He 'low, ' Well, you start ter go, kaze I seed you!' I say, ' Yes, an' I start ter come back, an' you'd 'a' seed dat ef you'd 'a' looked right close.' He 'low, ' 'Nervy, don't you know dem folks in yander'll think you b'long to um?' I say, ' I does. Ain't I free? Can't I b'long to um ef I wanter? I'd like ter see de one ter hender me. What dey done ter you? An' what's I done ter you dat you want ter drag me

'way fum my white folks? You go drag you'se'f—
you can't drag *me*.' He 'low, ' Dey done begin ter
call you a white-folks nigger, an' dey say you gwine
back on yo' own color.' "

Aunt Minervy Ann paused here to laugh. "Mad
ez I wuz, suh, de minnit Hamp said dat I know'd I
had ter change my chune. I 'low, ' I know right
pine-blank who tol' you dat. 'Twan't nobody in
de roun' worl' but ol' Cely Ensign, an' she ain't tell
you dat in comp'ny, needer. She tol' you whar nobody can't hear 'er but you. Don't you fret! des ez
soon ez I git thoo wid supper, I'm gwine 'roun' dar
an' drag 'er out an' gi' 'er de wuss frailin' any nigger ever got sence de overseers quit bizness. I ain't
fergot dat ar' possum you toted off ter her house.'

" Well, suh, I had 'im! He caved in. He 'low,
' 'Twan't no 'possum; 'twan't nothin' in de roun'
worl' but a late watermillion.' I holler, ' *Ah-yi!
watermillion!* Well, den, ef you want ter drag anybody off fum der white folks, go an' drag ol' Cely
Ensign—bekaze you can't drag me.'

" We jowered right smart, but I had Hamp in a
cornder. He went off an' stayed maybe a mont', an'
den he come back, an' atter 'while he got 'lected ter
de legislature. He done mighty well, suh. He got
nine dollars a day, an' ev'y Sat'dy night he'd fetch

de bigges' part uv it home. 'Twuz mighty handy, too, suh, kaze ef hadn't been fer dat legislatur' money I dunner what me and Miss Vallie an' Marse Tumlin would 'a' done.

" Dat wuz 'bout de time, suh, dat de town boys wanter ku-kluck Hamp, an' you an' Marse Tumlin went out an' ku-klucked dem. Hamp ain't never forgot it, suh. He'd walk fum here to Atlanty fer you ef 'twould do you any good. He don't say much, but I know how he feel. I hear 'im calling me now, suh."

" You haven't told me about Paul Conant," I suggested.

" I'll tell you, suh, 'fo' you go."

In half a minute I heard Aunt Minervy Ann quarrelling and laughing at Hamp in the same breath.

IV

HOW SHE JOINED THE GEORGIA LEGISLATURE

THE second day of the fair, I saw more of Paul Conant. He insisted on taking charge of me, and, in his buggy, we visited every part of the fair-grounds, which had been laid out on a most liberal scale. When dinner-time came I was glad enough to excuse myself and hurry back to the refreshing shade of Major Perdue's veranda. There I found Aunt Minervy Ann swinging the baby in a hammock.

" I 'low'd maybe you'd git tired an' come back, suh; an' so I des let dinner sorter simmer whiles I got dish yer baby ter sleep. I dunner how you all does in Atlanty, but down here we has soon dinner. Dem what wanter kin have two meals a day, but dem what does sho 'nuff work better eat three. Me! I want three, whedder I works er not."

The baby stirred, and Aunt Minervy paused. At that moment a group of men, wearing badges, passed by, evidently officials of the fair going to dinner. They were evidently engaged in a very earnest discussion.

" I'm for Conant," said one, with considerable emphasis.

" Oh, so am I," assented another. " When Jim told me this morning that he was a candidate for the Legislature, I told him flat and plain that I was for Paul Conant."

" That's right," remarked a third. " We want a man there with some business sense, and Conant's the man."

Aunt Minervy Ann laughed. " Ef de Legislatur' up dar in Atlanty is like it wuz when I b'long'd ter it, dey can't drag Marse Paul in dar; no, suh! dey can't drag him in dar."

Amazement must have shown in my face, for Aunt Minervy Ann immediately became solemn. " Ain't you never hear tell 'bout my j'inin' de Legislatur'? You may look an' you may laugh, but dat don't wipe out de trufe. Dey wuz a time when I jined de Legislatur' an' when I b'long'd ter de gang same ez Hamp did. You don't 'spute but what Hamp b'long'd ter de Legislatur', suh?" asked Aunt Minervy Ann, anxious to make out the title of her own membership. No, I didn't dispute

Hamp's credentials. He had been elected and he had served.

" I know'd you couldn't 'spute dat, suh," Aunt Minervy Ann went on, " 'kaze you wuz down dar when dey choosen'd 'im, an' you wuz dar when dem ar white folks come mighty nigh ku-kluckin' 'im; you wuz right dar wid Marse Tumlin an' Marse Bolivar. I never is ter fergit dat, suh, ner Hamp nudder; an' ef you don't b'lieve it, you des sen' us word you want us. Ef we git de word at midnight we'll git up, an' ef de railroad track is tore up we'll git a waggin, an' ef we can't git a waggin, we'll walk, but what we'll come."

" Well," said I, " tell us about your joining the Legislature."

" I may be long in tellin' it, suh, but 'tain't no long tale," replied Aunt Minervy Ann. " Atter Hamp come up here an' tuck his seat—dat what dey call it den, ef dey don't call it dat now—well, atter he come up an' been here some little time, I tuck notice dat he 'gun ter hol' his head mighty high; a little too high fer ter suit me. He want me ter go up dar wid 'im an' stay dar, 'kaze he sorter skittish 'bout comin' home when dem country boys mought be hangin' 'roun' de depot. But I up an' tol' 'im flat an' plain dat I wa'n't gwine ter

99

leave Miss Vallie an' let er' git usen ter strange niggers. I tol' 'im he mought go an' stay ef he want ter, but de fus' week he miss comin' home, I wuz gwine atter 'im, an' ef I fotch 'im home he won't go back in a hurry; I tol' 'im dat, flat an' plain.

"Well, suh, he done mighty well; I'll say dat fer 'im. He want too many clean shirts an' collars fer ter suit me, but he say he bleeze ter have um dar whar he at, an' I ain't make no complaint 'bout dat; but I took notice dat he wuz sorter offish wid Marse Tumlin. Mo' dan dat, I tuck notice dat needer Marse Tumlin ner Marse Bolivar so much ez look at 'im when dey pass 'im by. I know'd by dat dat sump'n wuz up.

"Now, Hamp ain't had no reg'lar time fer comin' home. Sometimes he'd come We'n'sday, an' den ag'in he'd come Friday. I ax 'im why he ain't stay de week out an' 'ten' ter his work like he oughter. He say he gettin' des much pay when he at home loafin' 'roun' ez he do when he up yer. Well, suh, dat 'stonish me. You know yo'se'f, suh, dat when folks is gittin' pay fer dat what dey ain't doin', dey's boun' ter be swindlin' gwine on some'rs, ef not wuss, an' dat what I tol' 'im. He laugh an' say dat's on account er politics an' de erpublican party, an' I make answer dat ef dat de case, dey er bofe rank an' rotten; desso.

"We went on fum one thing ter an'er, twel bimeby I ax 'im what dey is 'twixt 'im an' Marse Tumlin an' Marse Bolivar. Hamp say dey ain't nothin' 'ceppin' dat dey done ax 'im fer ter do sump'n dat ain't in 'cordance wid erpublican pencerpuls, an' he bleeze ter effuse um. Well, suh, dis kinder riled me. I know'd right pine-blank dat Hamp ain't know no mo' 'bout erpublican pencerpuls dan I is, an' I wouldn't a-know'd um ef I'd a met um in de road wid der name painted on um; so I ax 'im what erpublican pencerpuls hender'd 'im fum doin' what Marse Tumlin ax 'im ter do. He sot dar an' hummed an' haw'd, an' squirm'd in his cheer, an' chaw'd on de een' er his segyar. I wait long 'nuff, an' den I ax 'im ag'in. Well, suh, dat's been twenty years ago, an' he ain't never tol' me yit what dem erpublican pencerpuls wuz. I ain't flingin' off on um, suh. I 'speck dey wuz a bairlful er dem erpublican pencerpuls, an' maybe all good uns, but I know'd mighty well dat dey ain't hender dat nigger man fum doin' what Marse Tumlin ax 'im ter do.

"So de nex' chance I git, I up'n ax Marse Tumlin what de matter wuz 'twix' him an' Hamp. He

101

say 'twa'n't nothin' much, 'cep' dat Hamp had done come up here in Atlanta an' sol' hisse'f out to a passel er kyarpit-baggers what ain't no intruss down here but ter git han's on all de money in sight. I say, ' He may 'a' gi' hisse'f 'way, Marse Tumlin, but he sho' ain't sell hisse'f, 'kaze I ain't seen one er de money.' Marse Tumlin 'low, ' Well, anyhow, it don't make much diffunce, Minervy Ann. Dem kyarpit-baggers up dar, dey pat 'im on de back an' tell 'im he des ez good ez what dey is. I had de idee, Minervy Ann,' he say, ' dat Hamp wuz lots better dan what dey is, but he ain't; he des 'bout good ez dey is.'

" Marse Tumlin do like he don't wanter talk 'bout it, but dat ain't nigh satchify me. I say, ' Marse Tumlin, what did you want Hamp ter do? ' He drum on de arm er de cheer wid his fingers, an' sorter study. Den he say, ' Bein' it's all done an' over wid, I don't min' tellin' you all about it. Does you know who's a-runnin' dis county now? ' I had a kinder idee, but I say, ' Who, Marse Tumlin? ' He 'low, ' Mahlon Botts an' his br'er Mose; dey er runnin' de county, an' dey er ruinin' it.'

" Den he ax me ef I know de Bottses. Know um! I'd been a-knowin' um sence de year one, an'

dey wuz de ve'y drugs an' offscourin's er creation.
I ax Marse Tumlin how come dey ter have holt er
de county, an' he say dey make out dey wuz good
erpublicans, des ter make de niggers vote um in
office—so dey kin make money an' plunder de
county. Den I ax 'im what he want Hamp ter do.
He say all he want Hamp ter do wuz ter he'p 'im git
er whatyoumaycallum—yasser, dat's it, a bill; dat's
de ve'y word he say—he want Hamp ter he'p 'im
git a bill th'oo de Legislatur'; an' den he went on
an' tell me a long rigamarolious 'bout what 'twuz,
but I'll never tell you in de roun' worl'.''

[The proceedings of the Georgia Legislature re-
ported in the Atlanta *New Era*, of November 10,
1869, show that the measure in question was a local
bill to revive the polling-places in the militia dis-
tricts of the county represented by the Hon. Hampton Tumlin, and to regulate elections so that there
could be no repeating. This verification of Aunt
Minervy Ann's statement was made long ago after
she told the story, and purely out of curiosity. The
discussions shed an illuminating light over her narrative, but it is impossible to reproduce them here,
even in brief.]

" He tol' me dat, suh, an' den he le'nt back in de
cheer, an' kinder hummed a chune. An' me—I

stood up dar by de fireplace an' studied. Right
den an' dar I made up my min' ter one thing, an' I
ain't never change it, needer; I made up my min'
dat ef we wuz all gwine ter be free an' live in de
same neighborhoods—dat ef we wuz gwine ter do
dat, whatsomever wuz good fer de white folks
bleeze ter be good fer de niggers, an' whatsomever
wuz good fer Marse Tumlin an' Miss Vallie wuz des
ez good fer me an' Hamp.

" I 'low, ' Marse Tumlin, when you gwine up dar
whar Hamp at?' He say, ' Oh, I dunno; I'm tired
er de infernal place,' desso. Den he look at me
right hard. ' What make you ax?' sez he. I 'low,
' 'Kaze ef youer gwine right soon, I'm gwine wid
you.' He laugh an' say, ' What de dickunce you
gwine up dar fer?' I 'low, ' I gwine up dar fer ter
jine de Legislatur'. I ain't here tell dat dem what
jines hatter be baptize in runnin' water, an' ef dey
ain't, den I'll jine long wid Hamp.' Marse Tumlin say, ' You reckin Hamp would be glad fer to
see you, Minervy Ann?' I 'low, ' He better had
be, ef he know what good fer 'im.' Marse Tumlin say, ' Ef I wuz you, Minervy Ann, I wouldn't
go up dar spyin' atter Hamp. He'll like you none
de better fer it. De las' time I wuz up dar, Hamp
wuz havin' a mighty good time. Ef you know

what's good fer you, Minervy Ann, you won't go up dar a-doggin' atter Hamp.'

"Well, suh, right at dat time I had de idee dat Marse Tumlin wuz prankin' an' projeckin'; you know how he runs on; but he wa'n't no mo' prankin' dan what I am right now. (Nummine! I'll git back ter Hamp terreckly.) I laugh an' say, ' I ain't gwine ter dog atter Hamp, Marse Tumlin; I des wanter go up dar an' see how he gittin' on, an' fin' out how folks does when dey sets up dar in de Legislatur'. An' ef you'll put dat ar whatshisname—bill; dat's right, suh; bill wuz de word—ef you'll put dat ar bill in yo' pocket, I'll see what Hamp kin do wid it.' Marse Tumlin 'low, ' 'Tain't no use fer ter see Hamp, Minervy Ann. He done tol' me he can't do nothin'. I lef' de bill wid 'im.'

" I say, ' Marse Tumlin, you dunner nothin' 'tall 'bout Hamp. He must er change mighty sence dey 'fo' yistidy if he erfuse ter do what I tell 'im ter do. Ef dat de case, I'll go up dar an' frail 'im out an' come on back home an' ten' ter my work.'

" Marse Tumlin look at me wid his eyes half shot an' kinder laugh way down in his stomach. He 'low, ' Minervy Ann, I been livin' a long time, an' I been knowin' a heap er folks, but you er de bangin'est nigger I ever is see. Free ez you is, I wouldn't take two thousan' dollars fer you, cash money. I'll git Bolivar, an' we'll go up dar on de mornin' train. Vallie kin stay wid er aunt. 'Tain't gwine ter hurt you ter go; I want you ter see some things fer yo'se'f.'

"Well, suh, sho' 'nuff, de nex' mornin' me an' Marse Tumlin an' Marse Bolivar, we got on de train, an' put out, an' 'twa'n't long 'fo' we wuz pullin' in under de kyar-shed. Dat 'uz de fus' time I ever is been ter dis town, an' de racket an' de turmoil kinder tarrify me, but when I see 't'er folks gwine 'long 'tendin' ter der bizness, 'twa'n't no time 'fo' I tuck heart, 'kaze dar wuz Marse Tumlin an' Marse Bolivar right at me, an' dey wuz bowin' an' shakin' han's wid mos' eve'ybody dat come 'long. Dey wuz two mighty pop'lous white men, suh; you know dat yo'se'f.

"I 'speck de train must 'a' got in 'fo' de Legisla-tur' sot down, 'kaze when we went th'oo a narrer street an' turn inter de one what dey call Decatur, whar dey carry on all de devilment, I hear Marse Tumlin say dat we wuz 'bout a hour too soon. Right atter dat Marse Bolivar say, ' Tumlin, dat ar nigger man 'cross dar wid de gals is got a mighty familious look ter me; I done been seed 'im somewhar, sho'.' Marse Tumlin say, ' Dat's a fac'; I used ter know dat man some'rs.' Well, suh, I lookt de way dey wuz a-lookin', an' dar wuz Hamp! Yassar! Hamp! Hamp an' two mulatter gals. An' I wish you could 'a' seed um; I des wish you could! Dar wuz Hamp all diked out in his Sunday cloze which I tol' 'im p'intedly not ter w'ar while he workin' in de Legislatur'. He had a segyar in his mouf mos' ez big an' ez long ez a waggin-spoke, an' dar he wuz a-bowin' an' scrapin', an' scrapin' an' gigglin', an' de mulatter gals wuz gigglin' an' snickerin' an' squealin'—I *declaire*, Mr. Tumlin! you oughter be *'shame* er yo'se'f; oh, youer too *b-a-a-a-d!* ' "

With powers of mimicry unequalled, Aunt Minervy Ann illustrated the bowing and scraping of Hamp, and reproduced the shrill but not unmusical voices of the mulatto girls.

" I tell you de trufe, suh, whiles you could count ten you might 'a' pusht me over wid a straw, an' den, suh, my dander 'gun ter rise. I must 'a' show'd it in my looks, 'kaze Marse Tumlin laid his han' on my shoulder an' say, ' Don't kick up no racket, Minervy Ann; you got Hamp right whar you want 'im. You know what we come fer.' Well, suh, I hatter stan' dar an' swaller right hard a time er two, 'kaze I ain't got no use fer mulatters; to make um, you got ter spile good white blood an' good nigger blood, an' when dey er made dey got in um all dat's mean an' low down on bofe sides, an' ef dey yever is ter be saved, dey'll all hatter be baptize twice han' runnin'—once fer de white dat's in um, and once fer de black. De Bible mayn't sesso, but common-sense'll tell you dat much.

" Well, suh, I stood dar some little time watchin' Hamp's motions, an' he wuz makin' sech a big fool er hisse'f dat I des come mighty nigh laughin' out loud, but all dat time Marse Tumlin had de idee dat I wuz mad, an' when I start to'rds Hamp, wid my pairsol grabbed in de middle, he 'low, ' Min' yo' eye, Minervy Ann.' I walk up, I did, an' punch Hamp in de back wid de pairsol. Ef I'd 'a' hit 'im on de head wid a pile-driver, he couldn't 'a' been mo' dum'founder'd. He look like he wuz gwine th'oo de sidewalk. I say, ' When you git time, I'd like ter have a little chat wid you.' He 'low, ' Why, why '—an' wid dat he stuck de lit een' er his segyar in his mouf. Well, suh, you may b'lieve you done seed splutterin' an' splatterin', but you ain't never seed none like dat. He made a motion, Hamp did, like he wanter make me 'painted wid de mulatter gals, but I say, ' When you git

108

time fum yo' Legislatur', I got a sesso fer you ter
hear.'

"Wid dat, suh, I turn 'roun' an' cross de street
an' foller on atter Marse Tumlin an' Marse Bolivar.
I ain't mo'n git 'cross, 'fo' here come Hamp. He
'low, ' Why, honey, whyn't you tell me you wuz
comin'? When'd you come?' I say, ' Oh, I'm
honey, is I? Well, maybe you'll fin' a bee in de
comb.' He 'low, ' Whyn't you tell me you wuz
comin' so I kin meet you at de train?' I say, ' I
wanter see what kinder fambly you got in dis town.
An' I seed it! I seed it!'

"Well, suh, I 'speck I'd 'a' got mad ag'in, but
'bout dat time we cotch up wid Marse Tumlin an'
Marse Bolivar. Marse Tumlin turn 'roun', he did,
an' holler out, ' Well, ef here ain't Minervy Ann!
What you doin' up here, an' how did you lef' yo'
Miss Vallie?' He shuck han's des like he ain't see
me befo' in a mont', an' Marse Bolivar done de
same. I humor'd um, suh, but I ain't know what
dey wuz up ter fer long atterwards. Dey don't
want Hamp ter know dat I come 'long wid um.
Den dey went on, an' me an' Hamp went ter whar
he stay at.

"When I got 'im off by hisse'f, suh, he sot in ter
tellin' me how come 'im ter be wid dem ar gals, an'

he want me ter know um, an' he know mighty well
I'd like um—you know how men-folks does, suh.
But dey wa'n't na'er minit in no day dat yever
broke when Hamp kin fool me, an' he know'd it.
But I let 'im run on. Bimeby, when he get tired
er splanifyin', I 'low, ' What dat paper what Marse
Tumlin ax you ter put in de Legislatur'?' He say,
' How you know 'bout dat?' I 'low, ' I hear Marse
Tumlin tellin' Miss Vallie 'bout it, an' I hear Miss
Vallie wonder an' wonder what de matter wid you.'

" I fotch Miss Vallie in, suh, bekaze Hamp think
dey ain't nobody in de worl' like Miss Vallie. One
time, des 'fo' de big turmoil, when Marse Tumlin
hire Hamp fum de Myrick 'state, he fell sick, an'
Miss Vallie (she wa'n't nothin' but a school-gal
den) she got sorry fer 'im 'kaze he wuz a hired nigger, an' she'd fill a basket wid things fum de white
folks' table an' tote um to 'im. Mo' dan dat, she'd
set dar whiles he's eatin' an' ax 'bout his folks.
Atter dat, suh, de groun' whar Miss Vallie walk
wuz better'n any yuther groun' ter Hamp. So
when I call her name up, Hamp ain't say nothin'
fer long time.

" Den he shuck his head an' say dey ain't no use
talkin', he des can't put dat ar paper in de Legislatur'. He say ef he wuz ter, 'twon't do no good,

110

'kaze all de erpublicans would jump on it, an' den dey'd jump on him ter boot. I 'low, ' Whar you reckon I'll be whiles all dat jumpin' gwine on?' He say, ' You'll be on de outside, an' ef you wuz on de inside, dey'd hike you out.' ' An' who'd do de hikin'?' sez I. ' De surgeon er de armies,' sez he. ' White er black?' sez I. ' Yaller,' sez Hamp. I 'low, ' Good 'nuff; we'll see which un'll be hiked.' An' I told Hamp right den an' dar, dat ef he erfuse ter put dat paper in, I'll do it myse'f.

" Well, suh, whiles we settin' dar talkin', dey come a-rappin' at de do' an' in walk a big bushy-head mulatter, an' I ain't tellin' you no lie, he de mos' venomous-lookin' creetur you ever laid yo' eyes on. His ha'r wuz all spread out like a scourin' mop, an' he had a grin on 'im ez big ez dat gate dar. Hamp call 'im Arion Alperiar Ridley."

At this point I was compelled to come to the rescue of Aunt Minervy Ann's memory. The stateman's real name was Aaron Alpeora Bradley, and he was one of the most corrupt creatures of that corrupt era. He had a superficial education that only added to the density of his ignorance, but it gave him considerable influence with the negro members of the Legislature. Aunt Minervy Ann accepted the correction with alacrity.

"I fergot his name, suh, but I ain't never fergit him. He so mean-lookin' he make de col' chills run over me. He wuz a low-country mulatter, an' you know how dey talk. Eve'y time he look at me, he'd bow, an' de mo' he bowed de mo' I 'spized 'im. He call Hamp 'Mistooah Tummalin,' an' eve'y time he say sump'n', he'd gi' one er dem venomous grins. I declar' ter gracious, suh, I oughtn't ter talk 'bout dat man dis way, but de way he look wuz scan'lous. I done fergive 'im for dat long time 'go on 'count er what he done; but when I hear white folks 'busin' 'im in dat day an' time I know'd dey had mighty good groun', bekaze dey ain't no human kin look like dat man an' not be mean at bottom.

"Well, suh, Hamp, he up'n tol' dis yer Alpory er Alpiry (whatsomever his name mought be) what I come ter town fer, an' Alpory, he say, 'Mistooah Tummalin, you kyarn't do it. Hit would-er ruin you in de-er party, suh—er ruin you.' I kinder fired up at dat. I 'low, 'How come he can't do it? Ain't he free?' Ol' Alpory, he grin an' he talk, he talk an' he grin, but he ain't budge me. At de offstart I say ef Hamp don't put dat paper in de Legislatur', I'll put it in myse'f, an' at de windin' up I still say dat ef he don't put Marse Tumlin's paper

in de Legislatur', den I'll be de one ter do it. Ol'
Alpory say, 'You-er is got no marster, ma'am.'
Den I snapt 'im up an' cut 'im off short; I say, 'I
got one ef I want one. Ain't I free?' Den he
went on wid a whole passel er stuff dat I can't make
head er tail un, ner him needer, fer dat matter, twel
bimeby I say, 'Oh, hush up an' go on whar you
gwine.'

"Hamp look so broke up at dis dat I wuz kinder
sorry I say it, but dat's de only way ter deal wid
dem kind er folks, suh. Ol' Alpory wuz des fam-
ishin', suh, fer some un ter b'lieve he's a big
Ike; dat 'uz all de matter wid 'im an' I know'd it.
So he quit his jawin' when I snapped 'im up, an' he
sot dar some time lookin' like a cow does when her
cud don't rise. Bimeby he ax Hamp fer ter let 'im
see de paper what I want 'im ter put in de Legislatur'. He tuck it, he did, an' look at it sideways an'
upside down, an' eve'ywhichaway. Ez ef dat
wa'n't 'nuff, he took off his goggles an' wiped um
an' put um on ag'in, an' read de paper all over ag'in,
noddin' his head an' movin' his mouf, an' grinnin'.

"Atter he got th'oo, he fol' de paper up an' han'
it back ter Hamp. He say he can't see no harm in
it ter save his life, an' he 'low dat ef Hamp'll put it
in at one een' er de Legislatur', he'll put it in at de

't'er een'. Dey call one part a house, but nobody ain't never tell me, why dey call a wranglin' gang er men a house. Dey des might ez well call um a hoss an' buggy; eve'y bit an' grain. Well, suh, de house wuz de part what Hamp b'longs ter, an' de 't'er part wuz whar ol' Alpory b'long'd at, an' by de time dey wuz ready fer ter set in dar dey had e'en 'bout 'greed fer put de paper in at bofe een's.

" I went 'long wid Hamp, suh, an' he show'd me de way ter de gall'ry, an' I sot up dar an' look down on um, an' wonder why all un um, white an 'black, wa'n't at home yearnin' der livin' 'stidder bein' in dat place a-wranglin' an' callin' names, an' howlin' an' wavin' der arms an' han's. Dey wuz a big fat white man settin' up in de pulpit, an' he kep' on a-maulin' it wid a mallet. I dunner what his name wuz, but I hear one big buck nigger call 'im Mr. Cheer. Marse Tumlin tol' me atterwards dat de man wuz de speaker, but all de res' done lots mo' speakin' dan what he did; all un um 'cep' Hamp.

" Yasser; all un um 'cep' Hamp, an' he sot dar so still dat 'twa'n't long 'fo' I 'gun ter git shame un him. He sot dar an' fumble wid some papers, an' helt his head down, an' look like he skeer'd. I watch 'im, suh, twel I got so res'less in de min' I can't set still. Bimeby I got up an' went down ter

114

de front do'; I wuz gwine ter make my way in dar
whar Hamp wuz at, an' kinder fetch 'im out'n his
dreams, ef so be he wuz dreamin'. An' I'd a gone
in, but a nigger man at de do' barred de way. He
say, ' Who you want ter see?' I 'low, ' I wanter
see Hamp Tumlin, dat's who.' He say, ' Does you
mean de Honnerbul Hampton Tumlin?' I 'low,
' Yes, I does ef you wanter put it dat away. *Go in
dar an' tell 'im dat de Honnerbul Minervy Ann
Perdue is out here waitin' fer 'im, an' he better
come quick ef he know what good fer 'im.*'

" Wid dat, suh, I hear somebody laugh, an' look
up an' dar wuz Marse Tumlin standin' not fur fum
de do' talkin' wid an'er white man. He 'low,
' Scott, dis is Minervy Ann.   She got mo' sense an'
grit dan half de white folks you meet.'   Well, suh,
de man come up, he did, an' shuck han's an' say he
mighty glad ter see me.   I never is ter fergit his
name on 'count er what happen atterwards. 'Bout
dat time Hamp come out an' Marse Tumlin an' de
't'er man draw'd off up de hall.

" I say, ' Hamp, why in de name er goodness
ain't you 'ten' ter yo' bizness?   What you waitin'
fer?   Is you skeer'd?'   He vow an' declair' dat he
des waitin' a chance fer ter put de paper in.   I tol'
'im dat de way ter git a chance wuz ter make one,

115

an' wid dat he went on in, an' I went back in de gall'ry. Well, suh, 'twa'n't long 'fo' Hamp put in de paper. A man at de foot er de pulpit read it off, an' den a white man settin' not fur fum Hamp jump up an' say he want sump'n done wid it, I dunner what. Hamp say sump'n back at 'im, an' den de white man say he sorry fer ter see de honnerbul gemman gwine back on de erpublican party. Den Mose Bently—I know'd Mose mighty well—he riz an' say ef de erpublican party is got ter be led 'roun' by men like de one what des tuck his seat, it's high time fer honest folks ter turn der backs on it.

"Well, suh, when Mose say dat, I clap my han's, I did, an' holla 'Good! good! now you got it!' I couldn't he'p it fer ter save my life. De man in de pulpit maul de planks wid de mallet like he tryin' ter split um, an' he 'low dat ef folks in de gall'ry don't keep still, he'll have um cle'r'd out. I holla back at 'im, 'You better some er dat gang down dar cle'r'd out!' Quick ez a flash, suh, dat ar Mr. Scott what been talkin' wid Marse Tumlin jump up an' 'low, 'I secon's de motion!' De man in de pulpit say, 'What motion does de gemman fum Floyd secon'?' Den Mr. Scott fling his head back an' low, 'De Honnerbul Minervy Ann Perdue

116

done move dat de flo' be cle'r'd 'stidder de gall'ry. I secon's de motion.'

"Den fum dat he went on an' 'buze de erpublican party, speshually dat ar man what had de 'spute wid Hamp. Mr. Scott say dey got so little sense dat dey go ag'in a paper put in by one er der own party. He say he ain't keer nothin' 'tall 'bout de paper hisse'f, but he des wanter show um up fer what dey wuz.

"He totch'd um, suh, ez you may say, on de raw, an' when he git th'oo he say, ' Now, I hope de cheer will deal wid de motion of de Honnerbul Minervy Ann Perdue.' Mr. Scott say, ' She settin' up dar in de gall'ry an' she got des ez much right ter set on dis flo' ez nineteen out er twenty er dem settin' here.' De man in de pulpit look at me right hard, an' den he 'gun ter laugh. I say, ' You nee'n ter worry yo'se'f 'bout me. You better 'ten' ter dem ar half-drunk niggers an' po' white trash down dar. I wouldn't set wid 'em ef I never did fin' a place fer ter set at.'

"Wid dat, suh, I pickt up my pairsol an' make my way out, but ez I went I hear um whoopin' an' hollerin'."

"Well, they didn't pass the bill, did they?" I asked.

"What? dat paper er Marse Tumlin's? Bless yo' soul, suh, dey run'd over one an'er tryin' ter pass it. Mr. Scott fit it like he fightin' fire, an' make out he wuz terribly ag'in it, but dat des make um wuss. Hamp say dat inginer'lly dem ar laws has ter wait an' hang fire; but dey tuck up dat un, an' shove it th'oo. Dey tuck mo' time in de 't'er een' er de Legislatur', whar ol' Alpory wuz at, but it went th'oo when it start. I hope dey don't have no sech gwines-on now, suh. Ef dey does de whole county can't drag Paul Conant in dar. I'll jine um myse'f, 'fo' I'll let 'im git in dat kind er crowd."

V

HOW SHE WENT INTO BUSINESS

AUNT MINERVY ANN's picturesque reminiscences were sufficiently amusing to whet my appetite for more. The county fair, which was the occasion of my visit to Halcyondale, was still dragging its slow length along, but it had lost its interest for me. The displays in the various departments were as attractive as ever to those who saw them for the first time, but it seemed to me that all my old acquaintances, or their wives and daughters, had something on exhibition, and nothing must do but I must go around and admire it. A little of this goes far, and, as I had been through the various departments a dozen times over, I concluded that it would be more comfortable to remain away from the grounds altogether, making more room for those who desired to see the judges deliver the prizes, or who were anxious to witness the trotting matches and running races.

Therefore, when Major Tumlin Perdue (whose

119

guest I was) and his daughter, Mrs. Conant, made an early start for the fair grounds, on the fourth day, I excused myself, on the plea of having some letters to write. The excuse was readily accepted, especially by Major Perdue, who expressed a very strong hope that I would do the fair justice in the Atlanta newspapers.

" If you can put in a word about Paul Conant, I'd be glad if you'd do it," the Major added. " He's come mighty near working himself down to get the blamed thing a-going. If it wasn't on account of Paul, me and Valentine wouldn't go any closer to the fair grounds than we are right now. But we think maybe we can help Paul, and if we can't do that, we hope to keep him from running his legs off. He ain't well a bit. Vallie says he didn't sleep more than two hours last night for the pains in his shoulder."

" It seems to be an old trouble," I suggested.

"Yes, it's an old trouble," replied the Major. Then he looked over the treetops and sighed.

Here was the same air of mystery that I had observed when I first came, and I remembered that Aunt Minervy Ann had begun to tell me about it when she became entangled in her reminiscences. Therefore, when they were all gone, and Aunt

Minervy Ann had cleaned up the house and coaxed the Conant baby to sleep (which was no hard thing to do, he was such a fat and good-humored little rascal), I ventured to remind the old negress that she had neglected to tell me why the Major and his daughter were so mysteriously solicitous about Paul Conant's shoulder.

" Well, de goodness knows!" Aunt Minervy Ann exclaimed, with well-affected surprise; " ain't I done tell you 'bout dat? I sho' wuz dreamin', den, bekaze I had it right on de tip-eend er my tongue. I dunno what got de matter wid me deze days, less'n I'm gettin' ol' an' light-headed. Well, suh! an' I ain't tol' you 'bout dat!"

She paused, as if reflecting, but continued to rock the baby's cradle gently, moving it slower and slower, until, finally, she ceased to move it altogether. The baby merely gave a self-satisfied sigh, and settled into the profound and healthy sleep of infancy. Then Aunt Minervy Ann went out on the back porch, and seated herself on the top step. I followed, and found the rocking-chair I had occupied on a former occasion.

" I'll set here, suh, twel Hamp gits back wid de carriage, an' den I'll see 'bout gittin' dinner, an' he better make 'as'e, too, bekaze I ain't got no time ter

121

set here an' lis'n at dat baby, whiles he projickin'
out dar at dem groun's. I kin wait, suh, but I
can't wait all day."

"Major Perdue said that Mr. Conant's shoulder
was very painful last night," I suggested.

"Dat what Miss Vallie say, suh. She say dey
wuz up an' down wid 'im mighty nigh all night
long. I don't blame um, suh, but, dey ain't no use
talkin', grown folks kin be waited on twey dey er
sp'iled same ez chilluns. I'd cut my tongue out,
suh, 'fo' I'd say it ter anybody else, but I done got
ter b'lievin' dat Marse Paul Conant grunts an'
groans many a time des bekaze he wants somebody
fer ter worry wid 'im an' honey 'im up. I may be
doin' 'im wrong, suh, but I done get a sneakin' notion dat he's one er deze yer kinder menfolks what
likes to be much'd an' petted. An' dey'll do it, suh
—dey'll much 'im night er day, hot er col'. Des
let 'im say, ' Oh, my shoulder! ' an' bofe un um'll
try ter outdo de udder in takin' keer un 'im.

" Marse Tumlin is got mo' ways like a 'oman dan
any man I ever is laid eyes on. It's de Lord's trufe.
He ain't fussy like de common run er wimmen, but
his han' is des ez light an' his heart des ez saft ez
any 'oman dat ever breave de breff er life, let er
breave whence an' whar she mought. I look at 'im

"Oh, my shoulder!"

sometimes, an' I des nat'ally tease myse'f ter know how dat man kin stan' up an' shoot anybody like I done see 'im do. Hit's de same way wid Marse Bolivar Blasengame—you know him, I spec. Dey married sisters, suh, an' dey allers been monstus thick. Dem two wuz big dogs 'roun' here, suh, 'fo' de war. Ef you ain't never seed um in dem days, you never is ter know how folks looked up to um an' give way to um.

"But dey ain't put on no airs, suh. Dey des do like de quality all do. 'Taint money dat makes de quality; hit's dat ar kinder breedin' what'll make de finest folks stop an' shake han's wid a nigger des ez quick ez dey would wid de king er Rooshy—ef dey got any king dar. Long 'fo' de turmoil, suh, endurin' er de farmin' days, 'twuz des dat-a-way. When he 'uz at his richest, Marse Tumlin never did pass a nigger on de road, no matter how lonesome an' ragged he look, widout stoppin' an' axin' who he b'long ter, an' what he name, an' how he gittin' on. An' he allers gi' um sump'n, maybe a piece er terbacker, er maybe a thrip. I know, suh; I done hear my color talk, an' dey talks it down ter dis ve'y day. Dey ain't never been a time in dat man's life when he ain't think mo' er somebody else dan what he think er hisse'f. Dat's what I call de quality,

123

suh. 'Tain't money; 'tain't land; 'tain't fine duds; 'tain't nothin' 'tall like dat. I tell you, suh, dem what want ter be de quality is got ter have a long line er big graveyards behime um, an' dem graveyards is got ter be full er folks what use ter know how ter treat yuther folks. Well, suh, Marse Tumlin is got um behime him, an' dey retch fum here ter Ferginny an' furder. An' on dat account, he ain't 'shame' to show nobody dat he love um, an' he ain't afear'd ter tell nobody dat he hate um.

"I bet you right now, suh, ef you wuz ter ax Miss Vallie ef she ever see 'er pa mad, she'd look at you like she ain't know what you talkin' 'bout. Fum de time she has been born, suh, down ter dis ve'y day, she ain't never hear a cross word come from his mouf. She's seed 'im frownin' an' she's seed 'im frettin', but she ain't never hear no cross word. An' dat what make I say what I does. 'Taint nobody but de quality dat kin show der breedin' right in der own fambly."

"Why, I've heard that the Major has something of a temper," I remarked.

"*Temper!*" exclaimed Aunt Minervy Ann, holding up both hands; "temper, I hear you say! Well, suh, dat ain't no name fer it. I done seed bad men, but Marse Tumlin is de wuss man when

"Marse Tumlin never did pass a nigger on de road."

he git his dander up dat I yever come 'cross in all my born days. De fust time I seed 'im mad, suh, wuz right atter de folks come home fum der fightin' and battlin'. It make me open my eyes. I been livin' wid 'im all dem years, an' I never is know how servigrous dat man is.

"An' de funny part wuz, suh, dat he got mad 'bout a ole nigger 'oman." Aunt Minervy Ann paused to indulge in a very hearty laugh. "Yasser, all 'bout a ole nigger 'oman. In dem times we all had ter scuffle 'roun' right smart fer ter git vittles ter eat, let 'lone cloze ter w'ar. Miss Vallie wuz w'arin' a frock what her mammy had when she wuz a gal. An' de clof wuz right good an' look' mighty well on 'er. Ez fer me, I dunner whedder I had on any frock—ef I did 'twuz 'bout ter drap off'n me. 'Long 'bout dat time, court-week wuz comin' on, de fust court-week we had sence de folks come home fum battlin'. Dey wuz a great miration 'bout it, bekaze dey say ev'ybody gwine ter come an' see de lawyers rastle.

"Well, suh, it come 'cross my min' dat ef I kin bake some ginger-cakes an' make some chicken-pies, maybe I kin pick up a little money. De dime an' thrip species had all done gone, but dey wuz oodles er shin-plasters floatin' 'roun' ef you had

THE CHRONICLES OF AUNT MINERVY ANN

sump'n fer ter git um wid. I dunner whar in de worl' we got 'nuff flour an' 'lasses fer ter make de cakes. I know I got one chicken, an' Hamp he went off one night and borried two mo'. I ain't ax 'im whar he borry um, suh, bekaze 'twan't none er my business. We made de cakes, an' den we made de pies. Ef you ain't know how ter make um, suh, you'd be 'stonished ter know how fur dem ar chickens went. We made twelve pies ef we made one. Yasser! ez sho' ez I'm settin' here. We strung um out—a wing here, a piece er de back dar, an' a neck yonner. Twelve pies, suh, an' nuff chicken lef' over fer ter gi' Miss Vallie a right smart bait; an' de Lord knows she need it, an' need it bad.

" Well, suh, I make de ginger-cakes de week 'fo' court, bekaze it he'ps a ginger-cake ef you bake 'im an' den shet 'im up in a tight box whar he kin sweat, an' Monday we sot in ter bake de pies. I make de dough wid my own han's, an' I lef' Miss Vallie fer ter bake um, wid Hamp ter keep de fire gwine. De word wuz dat 'bout half-pas' ten Hamp wuz ter fetch me all de pies dey had ready, an' den go back fer de yuthers.

" I ain't say nothin' 'bout de balance er de cakes; bekaze I 'low'd ter myse'f dat I had 'nuff. I had many ez I kin tote widout gittin' tired, an' I ain't

"We made twelve pies ef we made one."

no baby when it comes ter totin' cakes. Well, suh, I been livin' a mighty long time, but I ain't never see folks wid such a cravin' fer ginger-cakes. Fum de word go dey wuz greedy fer 'm. Hit mought er been 'kaze dey wuz des natchally hongry, en den ag'in hit mought er been bekaze de cakes call up ol' times; but no matter 'bout dat, suh, dey des showered de shinplasters down on me. 'Twa'n't de country folks doin' de most er de buyin' at fust. It 'uz de town boys an' de clerks in de stores; an' mos' 'fo' I know'd it de cakes wuz all gone, an' Hamp ain't come wid de pies.

"I would 'a' waited, suh, but dey kep' callin' fer cakes so ravenous dat bimeby I crumpled my shinplasters up in a wad an' tuck my basket an' went pol-in' home fer ter hurry Hamp up. He wuz des git-tin' ready ter start when I got dar. I gi' Miss Vallie de money—you kin count it up yourse'f, suh; 'twuz fer fo' dozen ginger-cakes at a thrip a-piece—an' tol' her ter sen' Hamp atter some mo' flour an' 'lasses 'fo' night, 'kaze de ginger-cakes half-gone an' court-week ain't skacely open up. Hamp, he tuck de pies an' de cakes, an' I got me one er de low cheers out'n de kitchen, 'kaze I done tired er settin' on de een' uv a box.

"I 'speck you know right whar I sot at, suh;
127

'twuz dar by dat big chany-tree front er Sanford's sto'. Hit sho' wuz a mighty tree. De win' done blow'd up an' blew'd it down, but de stump stan'in' dar sproutin' right now. Well, suh, right under de shadder er dat tree, on de outer aidge er de sidewalk, I tuck my stan', an' I ain't been dar long 'fo' de folks 'gun ter swarm atter my cakes, an' den when dey seed my pies—well! hit look like dey fair dribble at de mouf.

" I sol' um all 'cep' one, an' ef I'd 'a' sol' dat un, I don't 'speck dey'd 'a' been any trouble; but you know what a fool a nigger kin be, suh, speshually a nigger 'oman. I tuck a notion in my min' dat I done so pow'ful well, I'd save dat pie fer Marse Tumlin an' Miss Vallie. So ev'y time somebody's come 'long an' want ter buy de pie, I'd up an' say it done sold.

" Bimeby, who should come 'long but dat ar Salem Birch! He dead now, but I 'speck you done hear talk un 'im, bekaze he made matters mighty hot in deze parts twel—twel—well, suh, twel he 'gun ter hone atter dat pie, ez you may say." Aunt Minervy Ann paused and rubbed her hands together, as if reflecting. Then she shook her head and laughed somewhat doubtfully.

" What dey want ter name 'im Salem fer, I'll

"I gi' Miss Vallie de money."

never tell you. Hit's a Bible name, an' mo' dan dat, hit's a church name. You know it yo'se'f, suh, bekaze dey's a Salem church not mo'n sev'm mile fum whar we settin' at right now. *Salem* Birch! Hit bangs my time how some folks kin go on—an' I ain't nothin' but a nigger. Dey's mo' chillun ruint by der names, suh, dan any udder way. I done notice it. Name one un um a Bible name, an' look like he bleedze ter go wrong. Name one un um atter some high an' mighty man, an' dey grows up wid des 'bout much sense ez a gate-post. I done watch um, suh.

" I 'speck dis yer Salem Birch would 'a' been a right good man but fer dat ar Bible name. Dat ruint 'im. I don't b'lieve dey's a man in de worl' what kin walk straight under dat name less'n he done been called fer ter be a preacher, an' Salem Birch ain't had no sech call up ter dat time. Dat much I know.

" Well, suh, dar sot de pie, an' dar wuz de ginger-cakes, ol' timers, big ter look at, but light ter handle. Eve'ybody want de pie, but my min' done made up. Some bought cakes stidder de pie, an' some des wipe der mouf an' go on. But, bimeby, here come Salem Birch, six feet high, an' his hat sot on de side er his haid like he done bought de whole town. I know'd de minnit I laid eyes on 'im dat he had dram in 'im, an' dat he wuz up ter some devilment. Him an' his bre'r, Bill-Tom, suh, had tarryfied de whole county. Dey wuz constant a-fightin', an' ef dey couldn't git nobody else ter fight, dey'd fight 'mongst deyse'f. Yassir! dem ar Birches had done whip der own daddy.

"An' yit, suh, dis yer Salem wa'n't no bad-lookin' man. He had long curly ha'r, an' he wuz constant a-laughin'. Ef de fac' troof wuz ter come out, I 'speck he had more devilment in 'im dan downright meanness; an' he wuz mean nuff, de Lord knows. But, be sech as it mought, bimeby here he come, sorter half tip-toein', like some folks do when dey feel der dram an' dunner how ter show it. He stop right front er me, suh, an' time his eye fell on me he sung out:

"'Whoopee! Ef here ain't ol' Minervy Ann! Wid pies! An' cakes! Come on, boys! Have some pies! An' cakes!'

"Well, suh, you mought er heer'd 'im a mile. He holler des like de She'ff do when he stick his haid out'n de court-house winder an' call somebody in ter court—des dat ve'y way. He say, 'How much you take fer yo' chicken-pie?' I 'low, 'Hit done sol', suh.' He say, 'I'll gi' you a quarter fer

130

"Ef here ain't ol' Minervy Ann wid pies!"

dat pie.' I 'low, ' De pie done sol', suh.' By dat
time dey wuz a right smart clump er folks come up
fer see what Salem Birch wuz holl'in' 'bout, an'
you know yo'se'f, suh, how a half-drunk man'll do
when dey's a crowd lis'nin' at him.

" He say, ' Who done bought dat pie?' I 'low,
' Marse Tumlin Perdue.' He sorter draw'd hisse'f
up, he did, an' say, ' Ain't I des ez good ez Tumlin
Perdue?' I 'low, ' I ain't know nothin' ter de con-
trary, suh, but ef you is, you got ter be a monstus
good man.' He say, ' I is! I'm de bes' man in de
county.' I 'low, ' Dat may be, suh; I ain't 'sputin'
it.' By dat time I 'gun ter feel de Ol' Boy kinder
ranklin' in my gizzard. He say, ' Why can't I git
dat pie?' I 'low, ' Bekaze it done sol', suh.' He
say, ' Fer cash?' I 'low, ' No, suh; but Marse
Tumlin's word is lots better'n some folks' money.'

" Well, suh, I know'd 'fo' I open my mouf dat I
ought'n ter say dat, but I couldn't he'p it fer ter
save my neck. He say, ' Well, blast yo' black hide,
my money's better'n anybody's money!' Wid dat
he flung down a shinplaster quarter an' retch fer de
pie. By de time he grabbed it, I grabbed it, an' he
pulled an' I pulled. I dunner whedder 'twuz de
strenk in me er de dram in 'im, but in de pullin', de
box what de pie wuz on turnt over, an' my cheer

turnt over, an' down come Salem Birch right spang on top er me.

"I tell you now, suh, dis skeer'd me. 'Twuz mo' dan I bargain fer. Right at de minnit, I had de idee dat de man had jumped on me an' wuz gwine ter kill me—you know how some folks is 'bout niggers. So I des give one squall——

"'Marse Tumlin! Run here, Marse Tumlin! He killin' me! Oh, Marse Tumlin!'

"Well, suh, dey tell me dat squall wuz so inhuman it made de country hosses break loose fum de racks. One white lady at de tavern hear it, an' she had ter be put ter bed. Bless yo' soul, honey! don't never say you done hear anybody blate twel you hear ol' Minervy Ann—an' de Lord knows I hope you won't never hear me.

"Dey ain't no use talkin', suh, hit 'larmed de town. Eve'ybody broke an' run to'rds de place whar de fuss come fum. Salem Birch got up des ez quick ez he kin, an' I wuz up des ez quick ez he wuz, an' by dat time my temper done run my skeer off, an' I des blazed out at him. What I say I'll never tell you, bekaze I wuz so mad I ain't never hear myse'f talk. Some say I called 'im dis an' some say I called 'im dat, but whatsomever 'twuz, hit wa'n't no nice name—I kin promise you dat.

"You see dat nigger 'oman?"

" 'Twus 'nuff ter rise his dand er, an' he draw'd back his arm fer ter hit me, but des 'bout dat time Marse Tumlin shoved 'im back. Marse Tumlin 'low, ' You dirty dog! You sneakin', nasty houn'! is dis de way you does yo' fightin'? '

" Well, suh, dis kinder skeer me ag'in, kaze I hear talk dat Salem Birch went 'bout wid dirks an' pistols on 'im, ready fer ter use um. He look at Marse Tumlin, an' his face got whiter an' whiter, an' he draw'd his breff, deep an' long.

" Marse Tumlin 'low, ' You see dat nigger 'oman? Well, ef she wuz blacker dan de hinges er hell '—he say dem ve'y words, suh—' ef she wuz blacker dan de hinges er hell, she'd be whiter dan you er any er yo' thievin' gang.' An' den, suh—I 'clar' I'm mos' shame ter tell you—Marse Tumlin rise up on his tip-toes an' spit in de man's face. Yasser! Right spang in his face. You may well look 'stonish'd, suh. But ef you'd 'a' seed de way Marse Tumlin looked you'd know why Salem Birch ain't raise his han' 'cep' ter wipe his face. Ef dey ever wuz blood an' killin' in anybody's eyes, hit wuz in Marse Tumlin's right dat minnit. He stan' dar while you kin count ten, an' den he snap his thumb an' turn on his heel, an' dat ar Salem Birch tuck'n walk 'cross de public squar' an' sot down on de court-house steps, an' he sot dar, suh, wid his haid 'twix' his han's fer I dunner how long.

" Well, suh, I know in reason dat de een' er dat business ain't come. You know how our white folks is; you kin spit in one man's face an' he not take it up, but some er his kinnery er his frien's is sho ter take it up. So I say ter myse'f, ' Look here, nigger 'oman, you better keep yo' mouf shot an' bofe eyes open, kaze dey gwine ter be hot times in deze diggin's.' When I come ter look at um, suh, my ginger-cakes wa'n't hurt, an' de chicken-pie wuz safe an' soun' 'cep' dat er little er de gravy had sorter run out. When I git thoo brushin' an' cleanin' um, I look up, I did, an' dar wuz Marse Bolivar Blasengame walkin' up an' down right close at me. You oughter know 'im, suh, him an' Marse Tumlin married sisters, an' dey wuz ez thick ez two peas in a pod. So I 'low, ' Won't you have a ginger-cake, Marse Bolivar? I'd offer you de pie, but I'm savin' dat fer Miss Vallie.' He say he don't b'lieve his appetite run ter cakes an' pies right dat minnit. Dat make me eye 'im, suh, an' he look like he mighty glum 'bout sump'n. He des walk up an' down, up an' down, wid his han's in his pockets. It come back ter me atterwards, but I ain't pay no 'tention den, dat de folks all 'roun'

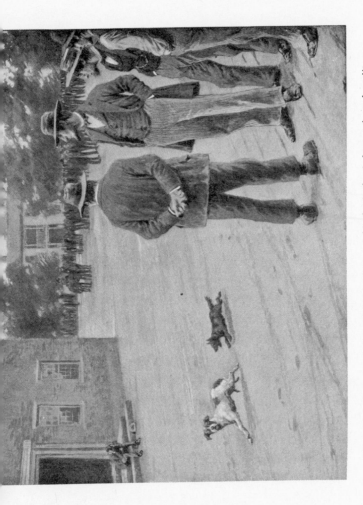

"An' he sot dar, suh, wid his haid 'twix' his han's fer I dunner how long."

town wuz kinder 'spectin' anudder fuss. Dey wuz all standin' in clumps here an' dar, some in de middle er de street, an' some on de sidewalks, but dey wa'n't nobody close ter me 'cep' Marse Bolivar. Look like dey wuz givin' us elbow room.

"De bigges' clump er folks, suh, wuz down at de public well, at de fur side er de squar', an' I notice dey kep' movin', now dis way, an' now dat, sorter swayin' like some un wuz shovin' um 'bout an' pushin' um 'roun'. An' dat des de way it wuz, 'kaze 'twa'n't long 'fo' somebody broke loose fum um an' come runnin' to'rds whar I wuz settin' at.

"I know'd in a minnit, suh, dat wuz Bill-Tom Birch. He wuz holdin' his han' on his wes'cut pocket fer ter keep his watch fum fallin' out. He come runnin' up, suh, an' he wuz so mad he wuz cryin'. His face wuz workin' des like it hurted 'im. He holler at me. 'Is you de ——?' I won't name de name what he call me, suh. But I know ef he'd 'a' been a nigger I'd 'a' got up fum dar an' brained 'im. I ain't say nothin'. I des sot dar an' look at 'im.

"Well, suh, he jerk a cowhide fum under his cloze—he had it run down his britches leg, an' say, 'I'll show you how you *erfuse* ter sell pies when a gemman want ter buy um.' I dunner what I'd 'a' done, suh, ef he'd 'a' hit me, but he ain't hit me. Marse Bolivar walk right 'twix' us an' 'low, ' You'll settle dis wid me, right here an' now.' Wid dat, Bill-Tom Birch step back an' say, ' Colonel, does you take it up?' Marse Bolivar 'low, ' Dat's what I'm here fer.' Bill-Tom Birch step back a little furder and make as ef ter draw his pistol, but his han' ain't got ter his pocket 'fo' *bang!* went Marse Bolivar's gun, an' down went Bill-Tom Birch, des like somebody tripped 'im up.

" I know mighty well, suh, dat I ain't no hard-hearted nigger—anybody what know me will tell you dat—but when dat man drapt, I ain't keer no mo' dan ef he'd 'a' been a mad dog. Dat's de Lord's trufe, ef I ever tol' it. I ain't know wharbouts de ball hit 'im, an' I wa'n't keerin'. Marse Bolivar ain't move out'n he tracks. He stood dar, he did, an' bresh de cap off'n de bairl what shot, an' fix it fer ter shoot ag'in. 'Twuz one er deze yer er-volvers, suh, what move up a notch er two when you pull de trigger.

" Well, suh, time de pistol went off, folks come runnin' fum eve'ywhars. Salem Birch, he come runnin' 'cross de public squar', bekaze he had de idee dat sump'n done happen. Marse Bolivar, he

"You'll settle dis wid me."

see Salem Birch a-comin', an' he walk out fum de crowd ter meet 'im. Dat make me feel sorter quare, kaze hit look like he wuz gwine ter shoot de man down. But Salem Birch seed 'im, an' he stop an' say, ' Colonel, what de name er God is de matter?' Marse Bolivar make answer, ' Salem, I had ter shoot yo' bre'r.' Salem Birch say, ' Is he dead?' Marse Bolivar 'spon', ' He ain't nigh dead. I put de ball 'twix' de hip an' de knee-j'int. He'll be up in a week.' Salem Birch say, ' Colonel, I thank you fer dat. Will you shake han's?' Marse Bolivar say dey ain't nothin' suit 'im better, bekaze he ain't got a thing ag'in' de Birches.

" An' 'twuz des like Marse Bolivar say. Bill-Tom Birch wuz wuss skeer'd dan hurt, an' 'twa'n't long 'fo' he wuz well. Salem Birch, he went off ter Texas, an' dem what been dar an' come back, say dat he's one er deze yer ervival preachers, gwine 'bout doin' good an' takin' up big collections. Dat what dey say, an' I hope it's des dat way. I don't begrudge nobody de money dey makes preachin' ter sinners, bekaze hit's des natchally w'arin' ter de flesh."   ,   ,

At this juncture Aunt Minervy Ann called to Hamp and informed him, in autocratic tones, that it was time to cut wood with which to cook dinner.

" I don't keer ef you is been ter de legislatur'," she added, " you better cut dat wood, an' cut it quick."

I suggested that she had started to tell me about Paul Conant's shoulder, but had neglected to do so.

" Ain't I tell you 'bout dat? Well, ef dat don't bang my time! Hamp, you hear dat? You better go an' make 'rangements fer ter have me put in de as'lum, bekaze I sho' I's gittin' light-headed. Well, suh, dat beats all! But I'll tell you 'bout it 'fo' you go back."

Then Aunt Minervy Ann went to see about dinner.

VI

HOW SHE AND MAJOR PERDUE FRAILED OUT THE GOSSETT BOYS

During the progress of the fair, there was some discussion of financial matters in Major Perdue's family. As I remember, someone had given Paul Conant a check which was thrown out by the Atlanta bank on which it was drawn. The sum was not a considerable one, but it was sufficiently large to attract Aunt Minervy Ann's attention.

"I 'speck dey got mo' banks in Atlanty dan what we-all got down here," she remarked, the next time I had an opportunity to talk with her. She laughed so heartily as she made the remark that I regarded her with some astonishment. "You may look, suh, but I ain't crazy. When I hear anybody say ' bank ' it allers puts me in min' er de time when me an' Marse Tumlin frailed out de Gossett boys."

"Frailed out the Gossett boys?" I exclaimed.

139

" Yasser, frailed is de word."

" But what has that to do with a bank?" I inquired.

" Hit got all ter do wid it, suh," she replied. We were in the sitting-room, and Aunt Minervy Ann sank down on a footstool and rested one arm on the lounge. " Right atter freedom dey wa'n't nothin' like no bank down whar we live at; you know dat yo'se'f, suh. Folks say dat banks kin run widout money, but 'fo' you start um, dey got ter have money, er sump'n dat look like money. An' atter freedom dey wa'n't no money 'roun' here 'cep' dat kin' what nobody ain't hankerin' atter.

" But bimeby it 'gun ter dribble in fum some'rs; fus' dem ar little shinplasters, an' den de bigger money come 'long. It kep' on dribblin' in an' dribblin' in twel atter while you could git a dollar here an' dar by workin' yo' han's off, er sprainin' yo' gizzard to git it. Bimeby de news got norated 'roun' dat ol' Joshaway Gossett gwine ter start a bank. Yasser! ol' Joshaway Gossett. Dat make folks open der eyes an' shake der head. I 'member de time, suh, when ol' Joshaway wuz runnin' a blacksmith shop out in de country. Den he sot in ter make waggins. Atter dat, he come ter be overseer fer Marse Bolivar Blasengame, but all de time he wuz overseein' he wuz runnin' de blacksmith shop an' de waggin fact'ry.

" When de war come on, suh, dey say dat ol' Joshaway tuck all de money what he been savin' an' change it inter gol'; de natchul stuff. An' he had a pile un it. He kep' dat up all endurin' er de turmoil, and by de time freedom come out he had mo' er de natchul stuff dan what Cyarter had oats. Dat what folks say, suh, an' when eve'ybody talk one way you may know dey ain't fur fum de trufe. Anyhow, de word went 'roun' dat ol' Joshaway gwine ter start a bank. Folks wa'n't 'stonished 'kaze he had money, but bekaze he gwine ter start a bank, an' he not much mo' dan knowin' B fum bullfoot. Some snicker, some laugh, an' some make fun er ol' Joshaway, but Marse Tumlin say dat ef he know how ter shave a note, he bleeze ter know how ter run a bank. I ain't never see nobody shave a note, suh, but dat 'zackly what Marse Tumlin say.

" But ol' Joshaway, he ain't a-keerin' what folks say. He start de bank, an' he kep' it up twel de time I'm gwine tell you 'bout. He bought 'im a big strong safe, an' he had it walled up in de back er de bank, an' dar 'twuz. Don't make no diffunce what folks say 'bout ol' Joshaway, dey can't say he

141

ain't honest. He gwine ter have what's his'n, an' he want yuther folks fer ter have what's der'n. When dat de case, 'tain't no trouble ter git folks ter trus' you. Dey put der money in ol' Joshaway's bank, whar he kin take keer un it, bekaze dey know'd he wa'n't gwine ter run off wid it.

"Well, suh, de bank wuz runnin' 'long des like 'twuz on skids, an' de skids greased. Ol' Joshaway ain't move ter town, but he hired 'im a clerk, an' de clerk stayed in de bank night an' day, an' I hear folks say de town wuz better'n bigger on 'count er ol' Joshaway's bank. I dunner how dey make dat out, 'kaze de bank wa'n't much bigger dan de kitchen back dar. Anyhow, dar she wuz, and dar she stayed fer a time an' a time.

"But one day Marse Tumlin Perdue tuck de notion dat he got ter borry some money. He seed yuther folks gwine in dar an' borryin' fum ol' Joshaway, an' he know he got des ez much bizness fer ter borry ez what dey is. Mo' dan dat, when he had plenty er money an' niggers, he done ol' Joshaway many a good turn. I know'd dat myse'f, suh, an' 'tain't no hearsay; I done seed it wid my own eyes. On de day I'm talkin' 'bout, Miss Vallie sont me up town fer ter ax Marse Tumlin kin he spar' two dollars—dat wuz befo' Miss Vallie wuz married; 'bout a mont' befo', an' she wuz makin' up her weddin' fixin's.

" 'Twa'n't no trouble ter fin' Marse Tumlin. He wuz settin' in de shade wid a passel er men. He seed me, he did, an' he come ter meet me. When I tell 'im what Miss Vallie want, he kinder scratch his head an' look sollum. He studied a minit, an' den he tell me ter come go 'long wid 'im. He cut 'cross de squar' an' went right ter ol' Joshaway's bank, me a-follerin' right at his heels. He went in, he did, an' 'low, ' Hello, Joshaway! ' Ol' Joshaway, he say, ' Howdy, Maje?' He wuz settin' in dar behime a counter what had wire palin's on top un it, an' he look fer all de worl' like some ongodly creetur what dey put in a cage for ter keep 'im fum doin' devilment.

" Marse Tumlin 'low, ' Joshaway, I want ter borry a hunderd dollars for a mont' er so.' Ol' Joshaway kinder change his cud er terbacker fum one side ter de yuther, an' cle'r up his th'oat. He say, ' Maje, right dis minit, I ain't got fifty dollars in de bank.' Nigger ez I is, I know'd dat wuz a lie, an' I couldn't help fum gruntin' ef I wuz gwine to be kilt fer it. At dat ol' Joshaway look up. Marse Tumlin stood dar drummin' on de counter. Bimeby ol' Joshaway say, ' Spoze'n I had it, Maje,

143

who you gwine git fer yo' skyority?' des so. Marse
Tumlin 'low, ' Fer my what?" ' Fer yo' skyority,' sez ol' Joshaway. I up an' say, ' Des lissen at
dat!' Marse Tumlin 'low, ' Who went yo' skyority when I use ter loan you money?' ' Times is
done change, Maje,' sez ol' Joshaway. Marse
Tumlin flirted de little gate open, an' went 'roun' in
dar so quick it made my head swim. He say, ' *I*
ain't change!' an' wid dat, he took ol' Joshaway
by de coat-collar an' cuff'd 'im 'roun' considerbul.
He ain't hurt ol' Joshaway much, but he call 'im
some names dat white folks don't fling at one an'er
widout dey's gwine ter be blood-lettin' in de neighborhoods.

"Den Marse Tumlin come out fum behime de
counter, an' stood in de do' an' look up town. By
dat time I wuz done out on de sidewalk, 'kaze I
don't want no pistol-hole in my hide. When it
come ter fa'r fis' an' skull, er a knock-down an'
drag-out scuffle, I'm wid you; I'm right dar; but
deze yer guns an' pistols what flash an' bang an'
put out yo' lights—an' maybe yo' liver—when it
come ter dem, I lots druther be on t'er side de
fence. Well, suh, I fully 'spected ol' Joshaway to
walk out atter Marse Tumlin wid de double-bairl
gun what I seed behime de counter; an' Marse

Tumlin 'spected it, too, 'kaze he walk up an' down befo' de bank, an' eve'y once in a while he'd jerk his wescut down in front like he tryin' ter t'ar de bindin' off. Bimeby I see Marse Bolivar Blasengame git up fum whar he settin' at, an' here he come, swingin' his gol'-head cane, an' sa'nt'in' 'long like he gwine on a promenade.

" I know'd by dat, suh, dat Marse Bolivar been watchin' Marse Tumlin's motions, an' he seed dat trouble er some kind wuz on han'. He walk up, he did, an' atter he cut his eye at Marse Tumlin, he turn ter me an' laugh ter hisse'f—he had de purtiest front teef you mos' ever is see, suh—an' he 'low, ' Well, dang my buttons, ef here ain't ol' Minervy Ann, de warhoss fum Wauhoo! Wharsomever dey's trouble, dar's de ol' warhoss fum Wauhoo.' Wid dat, he lock arms wid Marse Tumlin, an' dey march off down de street, me a-follerin'. You ain't kin fin' two men like dem anywhar an' eve'ywhar. Dey wa'n't no blood-kin—dey married sisters—but dey wuz lots closer dan br'ers. Hit one an' you'd hurt de yuther, an' den ef you wa'n't ready ter git in a scuffle wid two wil'-cats, you better leave town twel dey cool off.

" Well, suh, dey ain't took many steps 'fo' dey wuz laughin' an' jokin' des like two boys. Ez we

went up de street Marse Tumlin drapt in a sto' er
two an' tol' um dat ol' Joshaway Gossett vow'd dat
he ain't got fifty cash dollars in de bank. Dish
yer money news is de kin' what spreads, an' don't
you fergit it. It spread dat day des like powder
ketchin' fire an' 'twa'n't no time 'fo' you could see
folks runnin' 'cross de squar' des like dey er rabbit-
huntin', an' by dinner-time dey wa'n't no bank dar
no mo' dan a rabbit. Folks say dat ol' Joshaway
try mighty hard ter 'splain matters, but dem what
had der money in dar say dey'd take de spondulix
fus' an' listen ter de 'splainin' atterwards. 'Long
to'rds de noon-hour ol' Joshaway hatter fling up his
han's. All de ready money done gone, an' folks at
de do' hollin' fer dat what dey put in dar. I dunner how he ever got 'way fum dar, 'kaze dey wuz
men in dat crowd ripe ter kill 'im; but he sneaked
out an' went home, an' lef' some un else fer ter win'
up de shebang.

"De bank wuz des ez good ez any bank,
an' folks got back all dey put in dar des ez
soon ez dey'd let ol' Joshaway show his head
in town; but he drapt dat kinder bizness an'
went back ter farmin' an' note-shavin'. An'
all bekaze he want skyority fer Marse Tumlin, which his word des ez good ez his bon'.

He mought not er had de money when de clock struck de minit, but what diffunce do dat make when you know a man's des ez good ez gol'? Huh! no wonder dey broke ol' Joshaway down!"

Aunt Minervy Ann's indignation was a fine thing to behold. Her scorn of the man who wanted Major Perdue to put up security for his note was as keen and as bitter as it had been the day the episode occurred. She paused at this point as if her narrative had come to an end. Therefore, I put in a suggestion.

"Was this what you call frailing out the Gossett boys?"

"No, suh," she protested, with a laugh; "all deze yer gwines-on 'bout dat ar bank wuz des de 'casion un it. You bleeze ter know dem Gossett boys, suh. Dey had sorter cool down by de time you come here, but dey wuz still ripe fer any devilment dat come 'long. Dar wuz Rube an' Sam an' John Henry, an' a'er one un um wuz big ez a hoss. Dey use ter come ter town eve'y Chuseday an' Sat'day, an' by dinner-time dey'd be a-whoopin' an' hollin' in de streets, an' a-struttin' 'roun' mashin' folks' hats down on der eyes. Not all de folks, but some un um. An' all fer fun; dat what dey say.

147

" Tooby sho', dey had a spite ag'in Marse Tum-lin and Marse Bolivar atter de bank busted. Dey show'd it by gwine des so fur; dey'd fling out der hints; but dey kep' on de safe side, 'kaze Marse Tumlin wa'n't de man fer ter go 'roun' huntin' a fuss, ner needer wuz Marse Bolivar; but fetch a fuss an' lay it in der laps, ez you may say, an' dey'd play wid it an' dandle it, an' keep it fum ketchin' col.' Dey sho' would, suh. When dem Gossett boys'd come ter town, Marse Tumlin an' Marse Bolivar would des set' 'roun' watchin' um, des wait-in' twel dey cross de dead-line. But it seem like dey know des how fur ter go, an' right whar ter stop.

" Well, suh, it went on dis away fer I dunner how long, but bimeby, one day, our ol' cow got out, an' 'stidder hangin' 'roun' an' eatin' de grass in de streets like any yuther cow would 'a' done, she made a straight shoot fer de plantation whar she come fum.

Miss Vallie tol' Marse Tumlin 'bout it, an' he say he gwine atter her. Den some er de niggers in de nex' lot tol' me dat de cow wuz out an' gone, an' I put out atter her, too, not knowin' dat Marse Tumlin wuz gwine. He went de front street an' I went de back way. Ef de town wuz

big ez de streets is long, we'd have a mighty city
down here; you know dat yo'se'f, suh. De place
whar de back street jines in wid de big road is
mighty nigh a mile fum de tempunce hall, an'
when I got dar, dar wuz Marse Tumlin polin' 'long.
I holler an' ax 'im whar he gwine. He say he
gwine atter a glass er milk. Den he ax me whar
I gwine. I say I'm gwine atter dat ol' frame dat
nigh-sighted folks call a cow. He 'low dat he'd be
mighty thankful ef de nex' time I tuck a notion fer
ter turn de cow out I'd tell 'im befo'han' so he kin
run 'roun' an' head 'er off an' drive 'er back. He
wuz constant a-runnin' on dat away. He'd crack
his joke, suh, ef he dyin'.

" We went trudgin' 'long twel we come 'pon de
big hill dat leads down ter de town branch. You
know de place, suh. De hill mighty steep, an' on
bofe sides er de road der's a hedge er Cherrykee
roses; some folks calls um Chickasaw; but Chicky
er Cherry, dar dey wuz, growin' so thick a rabbit
can't hardly squeeze thoo um. On one side dey
wuz growin' right on de aidge uv a big gully, an'
at one place de groun' wuz kinder caved in, an' de
briar vines wuz swayin' over it.

" Well, suh, des ez we got on de hill-top, I hear a
buggy rattlin' an' den I hear laughin' an' cussin'.

149

I lookt 'roun', I did, an' dar wuz de Gossett boys,
two in de buggy an' one ridin' hossback; an' all un
um full er dram. I could tell dat by de way dey
wuz gwine on. You could hear um a mile, cussin'
one an'er fer eve'ything dey kin think un an' den
laughin' 'bout it. Sump'n tol' me dey wuz gwine
ter be a rumpus, bekaze three ter one wuz too good
a chance for de Gossett boys ter let go by. I dunner what make me do it, but when we got down de
hill a little piece, I stoop down, I did, an' got me a
good size rock.

"Terreckly here dey come. Dey kinder quiet
down when dey see me an' Marse Tumlin. Dey
driv up, dey did, an' driv on by, an' dis make me
b'lieve dat dey wuz gwine on 'bout der bizness an'
let we-all go on 'bout our'n, but dat idee wa'n't in
der head. Dey driv by, dey did, an' den dey pulled
up. We walkt on, an' Marse Tumlin lookt at um
mighty hard. Rube, he was drivin', an' ez we come
up even wid um, he 'low, ' Major Perdue, I hear tell
dat you slap my pa's face not so mighty long ago.'
Marse Tumlin say, ' I did, an' my han' ain't clean
yit.' He helt it out so dey kin see fer deyse'f. ' I
b'lieve,' sez Rube, ' I'll take a closer look at it.'
Wid dat he lipt out er de buggy, an' by de time he
hit de groun', Marse Tumlin had knockt 'im a-wind-

in' wid his curly-hick'ry walkin'-cane. By
dat time, John Henry had jumpt out'n de buggy,
an' he went at Marse Tumlin wid a dirk-knife. He
kep' de cane off'n his head by dodgin', but Marse
Tumlin hit a back lick an' knock de knife out'n his
han' an' den dey clincht. Den Rube got up, an'
start to'rds um on de run.

" Well, suh, I wuz skeer'd an' mad bofe. I seed
sump'n had ter be done, an' dat mighty quick; so I
tuck atter Rube, cotch 'm by de ellybows, shoved
'im ahead faster dan he wuz gwine, an' steer'd
'im right to'rds de caved-in place in de brier-bushes.
He tried mighty hard ter stop, but he wuz gwine
down hill, an' I had de Ol' Boy in me. I got 'im
close ter de place, suh, an' den I gi' 'm a shove, an'
inter de briers he went, head over heels. All dis
time I had de rock in my han'. By de time I turn
'roun' I see Sam a-comin'. When de rumpus start
up, his hoss shied an' made a break down de hill wid
'im, but he slew'd 'im 'roun', an' jumped off, an'
here he come back, his face red, his hat off, an' ol'
Nick hisse'f lookin' out'n his eyes. I know'd
mighty well I can't steer him inter no brier-bush,
an' so when he run by me I let 'im have de rock in
de burr er de year. 'Twa'n't no light lick, suh; I
wuz plum venomous by den; an' he went down des

151

like a beef does when you knock 'im in de head wid a ax."

Aunt Minervy Ann, all unconscious of her attitudes and gestures, had risen from the floor, and now stood in the middle of the room, tall, towering, and defiant.

"Den I run ter whar Marse Tumlin an' John Henry Gossett had been scufflin'; but by de time I got dar John Henry squalled out dat he had 'nuff; an' he wa'n't tellin' no lie, suh, fer Marse Tumlin had ketched his cane up short, an' he used it on dat man's face des like you see folks do wid ice-picks. He like to 'a' ruint 'im. But when he holla dat he got 'nuff, Marse Tumlin let 'im up. He let 'im up, he did, an' sorter step back. By dat time Rube wuz a-climbin' out'n de briers, an' Sam wuz makin' motions like he comin'-to. Marse Tumlin say, ' Lemme tell you cowardly rascals one thing. De nex' time a'er one un you bat his eye at me, I'm gwine ter put a hole right spang th'oo you. Ef you don't b'lieve it, you kin start ter battin' um right now.' Wid dat, he draw'd out his ervolver an' kinder played wid it. Rube say, ' We'll drap it, Major; we des had a little too much licker. But I'll not drap it wid dat nigger dar. I'll pay her fer dis day's work, an' I'll pay 'er well.'

" Well, suh, de way he say it set me on fire.   I stept out in de middle er de road, an' 'low, ' *Blast yo' rotten heart, ef you'll des walk out here I'll whip you in a fa'r fight.   Fight me wid yo' naked han's an' I'll eat you up, ef I hatter pizen myse'f ter do it.*' "

Once more Aunt Minervy Ann brought the whole scene mysteriously before me.   Her eyes gleamed ferociously, her body swayed, and her out-stretched arm trembled with the emotion she had resummoned from the past.   We were on the spot. The red hill-side, the hedges of Cherokee roses, Major Perdue grim and erect, Sam Gossett strug-gling to his feet, John Henry wiping his beaten face, Rube astounded at the unwonted violence of a negro woman, the buggy swerved to one side by the horse searching for grass—all these things came into view and slowly faded away.   Aunt Minervy Ann, suddenly recollecting herself, laughed sheep-ishly.

" I ain't tellin' you no lie, suh, dat ar Rube Gos-sett stood dar like de little boy dat de calf run over. He mought er had sump'n ugly ter say, but Marse Tumlin put in.   He 'low, ' Don't you fool yo'se'f 'bout dis nigger 'oman.   When you hit her you hits me.   Befo' you put yo' han' on 'er you come an'

spit in my face. You'll fin' dat lots de cheapes'
way er gittin' de dose what I got fer dem what
hurts Minervy Ann.'

"Well, suh, dis make me feel so funny dat a little mo' an' I'd a got ter whimperin', but I happen
ter look 'roun', an' dar wuz our ol' cow lookin' at
me over a low place in de briers. She done got in
de fiel' by a gap back up de road, an' dar she wuz
a-lookin' at us like she sorry. Wid me, suh, de
diffunce 'twixt laughin' an' cryin' ain't thicker dan
a fly's wing, an' when I see dat ol' cow lookin' like
she ready ter cry, I wuz bleeze to laugh. Marse
Tumlin look at me right hard, but I say, 'Marse
Tumlin, ol' June lis'nin' at us,' an' den *he* laughed.

"Dem Gossett boys brush deyse'f off good ez
dey kin an' den dey put out fer home. Soon ez
dey git out er sight, Marse Tumlin started in ter
projickin'. He walk all 'roun' me a time er two,
an' den he blow out his breff like folks does when
dey er kinder tired. He look at me, an' say, '*Well,
I be dam!*' 'Dat would 'a' been de word,' sez I,
'ef ol' Minervy Ann hadn't 'a' been here dis day
an' hour.' He shuck his head slow. 'You hit de
mark dat time,' sez he; 'ef you hadn't 'a' been here,
Minervy Ann, dem boys would sholy 'a' smasht
me; but ef I hadn't 'a' been here, I reely b'lieve
154

you'd 'a' frailed out de whole gang. You had two whipt, Minervy Ann, an' you wuz hankerin' fer de yuther one. I'll hatter sw'ar ter de facts 'fo' anybody'll b'lieve um.' I 'low ' 'Tain't no use ter tell nobody, Marse Tumlin. Folks think I'm bad 'nuff now.'

"But, *shoo!* Marse Tumlin would 'a' mighty nigh died ef he couldn't tell 'bout dat day's work. I ain't min' dat so much, but it got so dat when de Gossetts come ter town an' start ter prankin', de town boys 'ud call um by name, an' holla an' say, ' You better watch out dar! Minervy Ann Perdue comin' 'roun' de cornder! ' Dat wuz so errytatin', suh, dat it kyo'd um. Dey drapt der dram-drinkin' an' spreein', an' now dey er high in Horeb Church. Dey don't like me, suh, an' no wonder; but ef dey kin git ter hev'm widout likin' me, I'd be glad ter see um go.

"Well, suh, I call de ol' cow, an' she foller long on 'er side er de briers, an' when she got whar de gap wuz, she curl 'er tail over 'er back an' put out fer home, des for all de worl' like she glad 'kaze me an' Marse Tumlin frailed out de Gossett boys.

"I say, ' Marse Tumlin, I'm a member er de church an' I don't b'lieve in fightin', but ef we hadn't er fit wid dem Gossetts we'd 'a' never foun'

dat ol' cow in de roun' worl'.' He 'low, ' An' ef
we hadn't er fit wid um, Minervy Ann, I'd 'a' never
know'd who ter take wid me fer ter keep de booger-
man fum gittin' me.'

"Dat night, suh, Marse Bolivar Blasengame
come rappin' at my do'. Hamp wuz done gone ter
bed, an' I wuz fixin' ter go. Marse Bolivar come
in, he did, an' shuck han's wid me like he ain't seed
me sence de big war. Den he sot down over ag'in'
me an' look at me, an' make me tell 'im all 'bout
de rumpus. Well, suh, he got ter laughin', an' he
laughed twel he can't hardly set in de cheer. He
say, ' Minervy Ann, ef dem folks say a word ter
hurt yo' feelin's, don't tell Tumlin. Des come
a-runnin' ter me. He done had his han's on um,
an' now I want ter git mine on um.'

"Dat 'uz de way wid Marse Bolivar. He wa'n't
no great han' ter git in a row, but he wuz mighty
hard ter git out'n one when he got in. When he
start out he stop on de step an' say, ' Minervy Ann,
I didn't know you wuz sech a rank fighter.' ' I'm
a Perdue,' sez I. Wid dat he got ter laughin', an'
fur ez I kin hear 'im he wuz still a-laughin'. He
b'longed ter a mighty fine fambly, suh; you know
dat yo'se'f."

VII

MAJOR PERDUE'S BARGAIN

WHEN next I had an opportunity to talk with Aunt Minervy Ann, she indulged in a hearty laugh before saying a word, and it was some time before she found her voice.

" What is so funny to-day? " I inquired.

" Me, suh—nothin' tall 'bout me, an' 'tain't only ter-day, nudder. Hit's eve'y day sence I been big 'nuff fer to see myse'f in de spring branch. I laughed den, an' I laugh now eve'y time I see myse'f in my min'—ef I' got any min'. I wuz talkin' ter Hamp las' night an' tellin' 'im how I start in ter tell you sump'n 'bout Marse Paul Conant' shoulder, an' den eend up by tellin' you eve'ything else I know but dat.

" Hamp 'low, he did, ' Dat ain't nothin', bekaze when I ax you ter marry me, you start in an' tell me 'bout a nigger gal' cross dar in Jasper County, which she make promise fer ter marry a man an'

157

she crossed her heart; an' den when de time come she stood up an' marry 'im an' fin' out 'tain't de same man, but somebody what she ain't never see' befo'.'

" I 'speck dat's so, suh, bekaze dey wuz sump'n like dat happen in Jasper County. You know de Waters fambly—dey kep' race-hosses. Well, suh, 'twuz right on der plantation. Warren Waters tol' me 'bout dat hisse'f. He wuz de hoss-trainer, an' he 'uz right dar on de groun'. When de gal done married, she look up an' holler, ' You ain't my husban', bekaze I ain't make no promise fer ter marry you.' De man he laugh, an' say, ' Don't need no promise atter you done married.'

" Well, suh, dey say dat gal wuz skeer'd— skeer'd fer true. She sot an' look in de fire. De man sot an' look at 'er. She try ter slip out de do', an' he slipped wid 'er. She walked to'rds de big house, an' he walkt wid 'er. She come back, an' he come wid 'er. She run an' he run wid 'er. She cry an' he laugh at 'er. She dunner what to do. Bimeby she tuck a notion dat de man mought be de Ol' Boy hisse'f, an' she drapped down on her knees an' 'gun ter pray. Dis make de man restless; look like he frettin'. Den he 'gun ter shake like he havin' chill. Den he slip down out'n de cheer.

158

Den he got on his all-fours. Den his cloze drapped
off, an' bless gracious! dar he wuz, a great big black
shaggy dog wid a short chain roun' his neck. Some
un um flung a chunk of fire at 'im, an' he run out
howlin'.

"Dat wuz de last dey seed un 'im, suh. Dey
flung his cloze in de fire, an' dey make a blaze dat
come plum out'n de top er de chimbley stack. Dat
what make me tell Hamp 'bout it, suh. He ax me
fer ter marry 'im, an' I wan't so mighty sho' dat he
wan't de Ol' Boy."

"Well, that is queer, if true," said I, "but how
about Mr. Conant's crippled shoulder?"

"Oh, it's de trufe, suh. Warren Waters tol'
me dat out'n his own mouf, an' he wuz right dar.
I dunno but what de gal wuz some er his kinnery.
I don't min' tellin' you dat 'bout Marse Paul, suh,
but you mustn't let on 'bout it, bekaze Marse Tumlin an' Miss Vallie des' ez tetchous 'bout dat ez dey
kin be. I'd never git der fergivunce ef dey know'd
I was settin' down here tellin' 'bout dat.

"You know how 'twuz in dem days. De folks
what wuz de richest wuz de wussest off when de
army come home from battlin'. I done tol' you
'bout Marse Tumlin. He ain't had nothin' in de
roun' worl' but a whole passel er lan', an' me an'

Miss Vallie. I don't count Hamp, bekaze Hamp 'fuse ter b'lieve he's free twel he ramble 'roun' an' fin' out de patterollers ain't gwine ter take 'im up. Dat how come I had ter sell ginger-cakes an' chicken-pies dat time. De money I made at dat ain't last long, bekaze Marse Tumlin he been use' ter rich vittles, an' he went right down-town an' got a bottle er chow-chow, an' some olives, an' some sardines, an' some cheese, an' you know yo'se'f, suh, dat money ain't gwine ter las' when you buy dat kin' er doin's.

"Well, suh, we done mighty well whiles de money helt out, but 'tain't court-week all de time, an' when dat de case, money got ter come fum some'rs else 'sides sellin' cakes an' pies. Bimeby, Hamp he got work at de liberty stable, whar dey hire out hosses an' board um. I call it a hoss tavern, suh, but Hamp, he 'low its a liberty stable. Anyhow, he got work dar, an' dat sorter he'p out. Sometimes he'd growl bekaze I tuck his money fer ter he'p out my white folks, but when he got right mad I'd gi' Miss Vallie de wink, an' she'd say: 'Hampton, how'd you like ter have a little dram ter-night? You look like youer tired.' I could a-hugged 'er fer de way she done it, she 'uz dat cute. An' den Hamp, he'd grin an' 'low, 'I ain't

"Dat money ain't gwine ter las' when you buy
dat kin' er doin's."

honin' fer it, Miss Vallie, but 'twon't do me no harm, an' it may do me good.'

"An' den, suh, he'd set down, an' atter he got sorter warmed up wid de dram, he'd kinder roll his eye and 'low, 'Miss Vallie, she is a fine white 'oman!' Well, suh, 'tain't long 'fo' we had dat nigger man trained—done trained, bless yo' soul! One day Miss Vallie had ter go 'cross town, an' she went by de liberty stable whar Hamp wuz at, least-ways, he seed 'er some'rs; an' he come home dat night lookin' like he wuz feelin' bad. He 'fuse ter talk. Bimeby, atter he had his supper, he say, 'I seed Miss Vallie downtown ter-day. She wuz wid Miss Irene, an' dat 'ar frock she had on look mighty shabby.' I 'low, 'Well, it de bes' she got. She ain't got money like de Chippendales, an' Miss Irene don't keer how folks' cloze look. She too much quality fer dat.' Hamp say, 'Whyn't you take some er yo' money an' make Miss Vallie git er nice frock?' I 'low, 'Whar I got any money?' Hamp he hit his pocket an' say, 'You got it right here.'

"An' sho' 'nuff, suh, dat nigger man had a roll er money—mos' twenty dollars. Some hoss drovers had come 'long an' Hamp made dat money by trimmin' up de ol' mules dey had an' makin' um

161

look young. He's got de art er dat, suh, an' dey
paid 'im well. Dar wuz de money, but how wuz I
gwine ter git it in Miss Vallie's han'? I kin buy
vittles an' she not know whar dey come fum, but
when it come ter buyin' frocks—well, suh, hit
stumped me. Dey wan't but one way ter do it, an'
I done it. I make like I wuz mad. I tuck de
money an' went in de house dar whar Miss Vallie
wuz sewin' an' mendin'. I went stompin' in, I did,
an' when I got in I started my tune.

" I 'low, ' Ef de Perdues gwine ter go scandaliz-
in' deyse'f by trottin' down town in broad daylight
wid all kinder frocks on der back, I'm gwine 'way
fum here; an' I dun'ner but what I'll go anyhow.
'Tain't bekaze dey's any lack er money, fer here de
money right here.' Wid dat I slammed it down
on de table. ' Dar! take dat an' git you a frock
dat'll make you look like sump'n when you git outside er dis house. An' whiles you er gittin', git
sump'n for ter put on yo' head! ' "

Whether it was by reason of a certain dramatic
faculty inherent in her race that she was able to
summon emotions at will, or whether it was mere
unconscious reproduction, I am not prepared to say.
But certain it is that, in voice and gesture, in tone
and attitude, and in a certain passionate earnestness

Trimmin' Up de Ol' Mules.

of expression, Aunt Minervy Ann built up the whole scene before my eyes with such power that I seemed to have been present when it occurred. I felt as if she had conveyed me bodily into the room to become a witness of the episode. She went on, still with a frown on her face and a certain violence of tone and manner:

" I whipped 'roun' de room a time er two, pickin' up de cheers an' slammin' um down ag'in, an' knockin' things 'roun' like I wuz mad. Miss Vallie put her sewin' down an' lay her han' on de money. She 'low, ' What's dis, Aunt Minervy Ann?' I say, ' Hit's money, dat what 'tis—nothin' but nasty, stinkin' money! I wish dey wan't none in de worl' less'n I had a bairlful.' She sorter fumble at de money wid 'er fingers. You dunno, suh, how white an' purty an' weak her han' look ter me dat night. She 'low, ' Aunt Minervy Ann, I can't take dis.' I blaze' out at 'er, ' You don't haf'ter take it; you done got it! An' ef you don't keep it, I'll rake up eve'y rag an' scrap I got an' leave dis place. Now, you des' try me!' "

Again Aunt Minervy Ann summoned to her aid the passion of a moment that had passed away, and again I had the queer experience of seeming to witness the whole scene. She continued:

163

" Wid dat, I whipt out er de room an' out er de house an' went an' sot down out dar in my house whar Hamp was at. Hamp, he 'low, ' What she say?' I say, ' She ain't had time ter say nothin'— I come 'way fum dar.' He 'low, ' You ain't brung dat money back, is you?' I say: ' Does you think I'm a start naked fool?' He 'low: ' Kaze ef you is, I'll put it right spang in de fire here.'

" Well, suh, I sot dar some little time, but eve'ything wuz so still in de house, bein's Marse Tumlin done gone down town, dat I crope back an' crope in fer ter see what Miss Vallie doin'. Well, suh, she wuz cryin'—settin' dar cryin'. I 'low, ' Honey, is I say anything fer ter hurt yo' feelin's?' She blubber' out, ' You know you ain't!' an' den she cry good-fashion.

" Des 'bout dat time, who should come in but Marse Tumlin. He look at Miss Vallie an' den he look at me. He say, ' Valentine, what de matter?' I say, ' It's me! I'm de one! I made 'er cry. I done sump'n ter hurt 'er feelin's.' She 'low, ' 'Tain't so, an' you know it. I'm des cryin' bekaze you too good ter me.'

" Well, suh, I had ter git out er dar fer ter keep fum chokin'. Marse Tumlin foller me out, an' right here on de porch, he 'low, ' Minervy Ann,

"She wuz cryin'—settin' dar cryin'."

nex' time don't be so dam good to 'er.' I wuz doin'
some snifflin' myse'f 'bout dat time, an' I ain't keerin' what I say, so I stop an' flung back at 'im, ' *I'll
be des ez dam good ter 'er ez I please—I'm free!* '
Well, suh, stidder hittin' me, Marse Tumlin bust
out laughin', an' long atter dat he'd laugh eve'y
time he look at me, des like sump'n wuz ticklin' 'im
mighty nigh ter death.

" I 'speck he must er tol' 'bout dat cussin' part,
bekaze folks 'roun' here done got de idee dat I'm a
sassy an' bad-tempered 'oman. Ef I had ter work
fer my livin', suh, I boun' you I'd be a long time
findin' a place. Atter dat, Hamp, he got in de Legislatur', an' it sho wuz a money-makin' place. Den
we had eve'ything we wanted, an' mo' too, but
bimeby de Legislatur' gun out, an' den dar we wuz,
flat ez flounders, an' de white folks don't want ter
hire Hamp des kaze he been ter de Legislatur'; but
he got back in de liberty stable atter so long a time.
Yit 'twan't what you may call livin'.

" All dat time, I hear Marse Tumlin talkin' ter
Miss Vallie 'bout what he call his wil' lan'. He
say he got two thousan' acres down dar in de wire-
grass, an' ef he kin sell it, he be mighty glad ter do
so. Well, suh, one day, long to'rds night, a two-
hoss waggin driv' in at de side gate an' come in de

back-yard. Ol' Ben Sadler wuz drivin', an' he 'low, 'Heyo, Minervy Ann, whar you want deze goods drapped at?' I say, 'Hello yo'se'f, ef you wanter hello. What you got dar, an' who do it 'blong ter?' He 'low, 'Hit's goods fer Major Tumlin Perdue, an' whar does you want um drapped at?' Well, suh, I ain't know what ter say, but I run'd an' ax'd Miss Vallie, an' she say put um out anywheres 'roun' dar, kaze she dunner nothin' 'bout um. So ol' Ben Sadler, he put um out, an' when I come ter look at um, dey wuz a bairl er sump'n, an' a kaig er sump'n, an' a box er sump'n. De bairl shuck like it mought be 'lasses, an' de kaig shuck like it mought be dram, an' de box hefted like it mought be terbarker. An', sho' 'nuff, dat what dey wuz—a bairl er sorghum syr'p, an' a kaig er peach brandy, an' a box er plug terbarker.

"I say right den, an' Miss Vallie'll tell you de same, dat Marse Tumlin done gone an' swap off all his wil' lan', but Miss Vallie, she say no; he won't never think er sech a thing; but, bless yo' soul, suh, she wan't nothin' but a school-gal, you may say, an' she ain't know no mo' 'bout men folks dan what a weasel do. An den, right 'pon top er dat, here come a nigger boy leadin' a bob-tail hoss. When I see dat, I dez good ez know'd dat de wil' lan' done

166

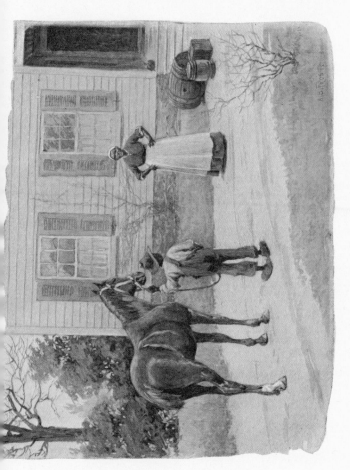

"Here come a nigger boy leadin' a bob-tail hoss."

been swap off, bekaze Marse Tumlin ain't got nothin' fer ter buy all dem things wid, an' I tell you
right now, suh, I wuz rank mad, kaze what we want
wid any ol' bob-tail hoss? De sorghum mought do,
an' de dram kin be put up wid, an' de terbarker got
some comfort in it, but what de name er goodness
we gwine ter do wid dat ol' hoss, when we ain't got
hardly 'nuff vittles fer ter feed ourse'f wid? Dat
what I ax Miss Vallie, an' she say right pine-blank
she dunno.

"Well, suh, it's de Lord's trufe, I wuz dat mad
I dunner what I say, an' I want keerin' nudder, bekaze I know how we had ter pinch an' squeeze fer
ter git 'long in dis house. But I went 'bout gittin'
supper, an' bimeby, Hamp, he come, an' I tol' 'im
'bout de ol' bob-tail hoss, an' he went out an' look
at 'im. Atter while, here he come back laughin'.
I say, ' You well ter laugh at dat ol' hoss.' He 'low,
' I ain't laughin' at de hoss. I'm laughin' at you.
Gal, dat de finest hoss what ever put foot on de
groun' in dis town. Dat's Marse Paul Conant's
trottin' hoss. He'll fetch fi' hunder'd dollars any
day. What he doin' here?' I up an' tol' 'im all
I know'd, an' he shuck his head; he 'low, ' Gal, you
lay low. Dey's sump'n n'er behime all dat.'

"What Hamp say sorter make me put on my

studyin'-cap; but when you come ter look at it, suh, dey wan't nothin' 'tall fer me ter study 'bout. All I had ter do wuz ter try ter fin' out what wuz be-hime it, an' let it go at dat. When Marse Tumlin come home ter supper, I know'd sump'n wuz de matter wid 'im. I know'd it by his looks, suh. It's sorter wid folks like 'tis wid chillun. Ef you keer sump'n 'bout um you'll watch der motions, and ef you watch der motions dey don't hatter tell you when sump'n de matter. He come in so easy, suh, dat Miss Vallie ain't hear 'im, but I hear de do' screak, an' I know'd 'twuz him. We wuz talkin' an' gwine on at a mighty rate, an' I know'd he done stop ter lisn'.

" Miss Vallie, she 'low she 'speck somebody made 'im a present er dem ar things. I say, ' Uh-uh, honey! don't you fool yo'se'f. Nobody ain't gwine ter do dat. Our folks ain't no mo' like dey useter wuz, dan crabapples is like plums. Dey done come ter dat pass dat whatsomever dey gits der han's on dey 'fuse ter turn it loose. All un um, 'cep' Marse Tumlin Perdue. Dey ain't no tell-in' what he gun fer all dat trash. *Trash!* Hit's wuss'n trash! I wish you'd go out dar an' look at dat ol' bob-tail hoss. Why dat ol' hoss wuz stove up long 'fo' de war. By rights he ought ter be in

de bone-yard dis ve'y minnit. He won't be here
two whole days 'fo' you'll see de buzzards lined up
out dar on de back fence waitin', an' dey won't hatter wait long nudder. Ef dey sen' any corn here
fer ter feed dat bag er bones wid, I'll parch it an'
eat it myse'f 'fo' he shill have it. Ef anybody
'speck I'm gwine ter 'ten' ter dat ol' frame, deyer
'speckin' wid de wrong specks. I tell you dat right
now.'

"All dis time Marse Tumlin wuz stan'in' out in
de hall lis'nin'. Miss Vallie talk mighty sweet
'bout it. She say, ' Ef dey ain't nobody else ter
'ten' de hoss, reckin I kin do it.' I 'low, ' My life
er me, honey! de nex' news you know you'll be
hirin' out ter de liberty stable.'

"Well, suh, my talk 'gun ter git so hot dat Marse
Tumlin des had ter make a fuss. He fumbled wid
de do' knob, an' den come walkin' down de hall, an'
by dat time I wuz in de dinin'-room. I walk
mighty light, bekaze ef he say anything I want ter
hear it. You can't call it eave-drappin', suh; hit
look ter me dat 'twuz ez much my business ez 'twuz
dern, an' I ain't never got dat idee out'n my head
down ter dis day.

"But Marse Tumlin ain't say nothin', 'cep' fer
ter ax Miss Vallie ef she feelin' well, an' how eve'y-

thing wuz, but de minnit I hear 'im open his mouf I know'd he had trouble on his min'. I can't tell you how I know'd it, suh, but dar 'twuz. Look like he tried to hide it, bekaze he tol' a whole lot of funny tales 'bout folks, an' 'twan't long befo' he had Miss Vallie laughin' fit ter kill. But he ain't fool me, suh.

" Bimeby, Miss Vallie, she come in de dinin'-room fer ter look atter settin' de table, bekaze fum a little gal she allers like ter have de dishes fix des so. She wuz sorter hummin' a chune, like she ain't want' ter talk, but I ain't let dat stan' in my way.

" I 'low,' I wish eve'ybody wuz like dat Mr. Paul Conant. I bet you right now he been down town dar all day makin' money han' over fist, des ez fast ez he can rake it in. I know it, kaze I does his washin' and cleans up his room fer 'im.'

" Miss Vallie say, ' Well, what uv it? Money don't make 'im no better'n anybody else.' I 'low, ' Hit don't make 'im no wuss; an' den, 'sides dat, he ain't gwine ter let nobody swindle 'im.'

" By dat time, I hatter go out an' fetch supper in, an' 'tain't take me no time, bekaze I wuz des' achin' fer ter hear how Marse Tumlin come by dem ar contraptions an' contrivances. An' I stayed in

170

dar ter wait on de table, which it ain't need no waitin' on.

"Atter while, I 'low, ' Marse Tumlin, I like ter forgot ter tell you—yo' things done come.' He say, ' What things, Minervy Ann?' I 'low, ' Dem ar contraptions, an' dat ar bob-tail hoss. He look mighty lean an' hongry, de hoss do, but Hamp he say dat's bekaze he's a high-bred hoss. He say dem ar high-bred hosses won't take on no fat, no matter how much you feed um.'

"Marse Tumlin sorter drum on de table. Atter while he 'low, ' Dey done come, is dey, Minervy Ann?' I say, ' Yasser, dey er here right now. Hamp puts it down dat dat ar hoss one er de gayliest creatur's what ever make a track in dis town.'

"Well, suh, 'tain't no use ter tell you what else wuz said, kaze 'twan't much. I seed dat Marse Tumlin want gwine ter talk 'bout it, on account er bein' 'fear'd he'd hurt Miss Vallie's feelin's ef he tol' 'er dat he done swap off all dat wil' lan' fer dem ar things an' dat ar bob-tail hoss. Dat what he done. Yasser! I hear 'im sesso atterwards. He swap it off ter Marse Paul Conant.

"I thank my Lord it come out all right, but it come mighty nigh bein' de ruination er de fambly."

"How was that?" I inquired.

" Dat what I'm gwine ter tell you, suh. Right atter supper dat night, Marse Tumlin say he got ter go down town fer ter see a man on some business, an' he ax me ef I won't stay in de house dar wid Miss Vallie. 'Twa'n't no trouble ter me, bekaze I'd 'a' been on de place anyhow, an' so when I got de kitchen cleaned up an' de things put away, I went back in de house whar Miss Vallie wuz at. Marse Tumlin wuz done gone.

" Miss Vallie, she sot at de table doin' some kind er rufflin', an' I sot back ag'in de wall in one er dem ar high-back cheers. What we said I'll never tell you, suh, bekaze I'm one er deze kinder folks what ain't no sooner set down an' git still dan dey goes ter noddin'. Dat's me. Set me down in a cheer, high-back er low-back, an' I'm done gone! I kin set here on de step an' keep des ez wide-'wake ez a skeer'd rabbit, but set me down in a cheer—well, suh, I'd like ter see anybody keep me 'wake when dat's de case.

" Dar I sot in dat ar high-back cheer, Miss Vallie rufflin' an' flutin' sump'n, an' tryin' ter make me talk, an' my head rollin' 'roun' like my neck done broke. Bimeby, *blam! blam!* come on de do'. We got one er dem ar jinglin' bells now, suh, but in dem times we had a knocker, an' it soun' like de

"He been axin' me lots 'bout Miss Vallie."

roof fallin' in. I like ter jumped out'n my skin. Miss Vallie drapped her conflutements an' 'low, ' What in de worl'! Aunt Minervy Ann, go ter de do'.'

" Well, suh, I went, but I ain't had no heart in it, bekaze I ain't know who it mought be, an' whar dey come fum, an' what dey want. But I went. 'Twuz me er Miss Vallie, an' I want gwine ter let dat chile go, not dat time er night, dough 'twa'n't so mighty late.

" I open de do' on de crack, I did, an' 'low, ' Who dat?' Somebody make answer, ' Is de Major in, Aunt Minervy Ann?' an' I know'd right den it wuz Marse Paul Conant. An' it come over me dat he had sump'n ter do wid sendin' er dem contraptions, mo' 'speshually dat ar bob-tail hoss. An' den, too, suh, lots quicker'n I kin tell it, hit come over me dat he been axin' me lots 'bout Miss Vallie. All come 'cross my min', suh, whiles I pullin' de do' open.

" I 'low, I did, ' No, suh; Marse Tumlin gone down town fer ter look atter some business, but he sho ter come back terreckly. Won't you come in, suh, an' wait fer 'im?' He sorter flung his head back an' laugh, saft like, an' say, ' I don't keer ef I do, Aunt Minervy Ann.'

"I 'low, ' Walk right in de parlor, suh, an' I'll make a light mos' 'fo' you kin turn 'roun'. He come in, he did, an' I lit de lamp, an' time I lit 'er she 'gun ter smoke. Well, suh, he tuck dat lamp, run de wick up an' down a time er two, an' dar she wuz, bright ez day.

"When I went back in de room whar Miss Vallie wuz at, she wuz stan'in' dar lookin' skeer'd. She say, ' Who dat?' I 'low, ' Hit's Marse Paul Conant, dat's who 'tis. She say, ' What he want?' I 'low, ' Nothin' much; he does come a-courtin'. Better jump up an' not keep 'im waitin'.'

"Well, suh, you could 'a' knock'd 'er down wid a fedder. She stood dar wid 'er han' on 'er th'oat takin' short breffs, des like a little bird does when it flies in de winder an' dunner how ter fly out ag'in.

"Bimeby, she say, ' Aunt Minervy Ann, you ought ter be 'shame or yo'se'f! I know dat man when I see 'im, an' dat's all.' I 'low, ' Honey, you know mighty well he ain't come callin'. But he wanter see Marse Tumlin, an' dey ain't nothin' fer ter hender you fum gwine in dar an' makin' 'im feel at home while's he waitin'.' She sorter study awhile, an' den she blush up. She say, ' I dunno whedder I ought ter.'

"Well, suh, dat settled it. I know'd by de way

174

she look an' talk dat she don't need no mo' 'swadin'.
I say, 'All right, honey, do ez you please; but it's
yo' house; you er de mist'iss; an' it'll look mighty
funny ef dat young man got ter set in dar by hisse'f
an' look at de wall whiles he waitin' fer Marse Tumlin.   I dunner what he'll say, kaze I ain't never
hear 'im talk 'bout nobody; but I know mighty well
he'll do a heap er thinkin'.'

"Des like I tell you, suh—she skipped 'roun'
dar, an' flung on 'er Sunday frock, shuck out 'er
curls, an' sorter fumble' 'roun' wid some ribbons,
an' dar she wuz, lookin' des ez fine ez a fiddle, ef not
finer.   Den she swep' inter de parlor, an', you
mayn't b'lieve it, suh, but she mighty nigh tuck de
man's breff 'way.   Mon, she wuz purty, an' she
ain't do no mo' like deze eve'y-day gals dan nothin'.
When she start 'way fum me, she wuz a gal.   By
de time she walk up de hall an' sweep in dat parlor,
she wuz a grown 'oman.   De blush what she had
on at fust stayed wid 'er an' look like 't wuz er
natchual color, an' her eyes shine, suh, like she had
fire in um.   I peeped at 'er, suh, fum behime de cur-
tains in de settin'-room, an' I know what I'm talkin' 'bout.   It's de Lord's trufe, suh, ef de men folks
could tote derse'f like de wimmen, an' do one way
whiles dey feelin' annuder way, dey wouldn't be no
175

livin' in de worl'. You take a school gal, suh, an'
she kin fool de smartest man what ever trod shoe
leather. He may talk wid 'er all day an' half de
night, an' he never is ter fin' out what she thinkin'
'bout. Sometimes de gals fools deyse'f, suh, but
dat's mighty seldom.

"I dunner what all dey say, kaze I ain't been in
dar so mighty long 'fo' I wuz noddin', but I did
hear Marse Paul say he des drapt in fer 'pollygize
'bout a little joke he played on Marse Tumlin. Miss
Vallie ax what wuz de joke, an' he 'low dat Marse
Tumlin wuz banterin' folks fer ter buy his wil'
lan'; an' Marse Paul ax 'im what he take fer it, an'
Marse Tumlin 'low he'll take anything what he can
chaw, sop, er drink. Dem wuz de words—chaw,
sop, er drink. Wid dat, Marse Paul say he'd gi'
'im a box er terbarker, a bairl er syr'p, an' a kaig er
peach brandy an' th'ow in his buggy-hoss fer good
medjer. Marse Tumlin say ' done ' an' dey shuck
han's on it. Dat what Marse Paul tol' Miss Vallie,
an he 'low he des done it fer fun, kaze he done
looked inter dat wil' lan', an' he 'low she's wuff a
pile er money.

"Well, suh, 'bout dat time, I 'gun ter nod, an'
de fus news I know'd Miss Vallie wuz whackin'
'way on de peanner, an' it look like ter me she wuz

des tryin' 'erse'f. By dat time, dey wuz gettin' right chummy, an' so I des curl up on de flo', an' dream dat de peanner chunes wuz comin' out'n a bairl des like 'lasses.

"When I waked up, Marse Paul Conant done gone, an' Marse Tumlin ain't come, an' Miss Vallie wuz settin' dar in de parlor lookin' up at de ceilin' like she got some mighty long thoughts. Her color wuz still up. I look at 'er an' laugh, an' she made a mouf at me, an' I say ter myse'f, 'Hey! sump'n de matter here, sho,' but I say out loud, 'Marse Paul Conant sho gwine ter ax me ef you ain't had a dram.' She laugh an' say, 'What answer you gwine ter make?' I 'low, 'I'll bow an' say, " No, suh; I'm de one dat drinks all de dram fer de fambly."'

"Well, suh, dat chile sot in ter laughin', an' she laugh an' laugh twel she went inter highsterics. She wuz keyed up too high, ez you mought say, an' dat's de way she come down ag'in. Bimeby, Marse Tumlin come, an' Miss Vallie, she tol' 'm 'bout how Marse Paul done been dar; an' he sot dar, he did, an' hummed an' haw'd, an' done so funny dat, bimeby, I 'low, 'Well, folks, I'll hatter tell you good-night,' an' wid dat I went out."

At this point Aunt Minervy leaned forward,

177

clasped her hands over her knees, and shook her head. When she took up the thread of her narrative, if it can be called such, the tone of her voice was more subdued, almost confidential, in fact.

" Nex' mornin' wuz my wash-day, suh, an' 'bout ten o'clock, when I got ready, dey want no bluin' in de house an' mighty little soap. I hunted high an' I hunted low, but no bluin' kin I fin'. An' dat make me mad, bekaze ef I hatter go down town atter de bluin', my wash-day'll be broke inter. But 'tain't no good fer ter git mad, bekaze I wuz bleeze ter go atter de bluin'. So I tighten up my head-hankcher, an' flung a cape on my shoulders an' put out.

" I 'speck you know how 'tis, suh. You can't go down town but what you'll see nigger wimmen stan'in' out in de front yards lookin' over de palin's. Dey all know'd me an' I know'd dem, an' de las' blessed one un um hatter hail me ez I go by, an' I hatter stop an' pass de time er day, kaze ef I'd 'a' whipt on by, dey'd 'a' said I wuz gwine back bofe on my church an' on my color. I dunner how long dey kep' me, but time I got ter Proctor's sto', I know'd I'd been on de way too long.

" I notice a crowd er men out dar, some settin' an' some stan'in', but I run'd in, I did, an' de young

"I hatter stop an' pass de time er day."

man what do de clerkin', he foller me in an' ax what
I want. I say I want a dime's wuff er bluin', an'
fer ter please, suh, wrop it up des ez quick ez he kin.
I tuck notice dat while he wuz gittin' it out'n de
box, he sorter stop like he lis'nin' an' den ag'in,
whiles he had it in de scoop des ready fer ter drap
it in de scales, he helt his han' an' wait. Den I
know'd he wuz lis'nin'.

"Dat makes me lis'n, an' den I hear Marse Tumlin talkin', an' time I hear 'im I know'd he wuz er-
rytated. Twa'n't bekaze he wuz talkin' loud, suh,
but 'twuz bekaze he wuz talkin' level. When he
talk loud, he feelin' good. When he talk low, an'
one word soun' same ez anudder, den somebody
better git out'n his way. I lef' de counter an' step
ter de do' fer ter see what de matter wuz betwix'
um.

"Well, suh, dar wuz Marse Tumlin stan'in' dar
close ter Tom Perryman. Marse Tumlin, 'low,
'Maybe de law done 'pinted you my gyardeen.
How you know I been swindled?' Tom Perryman say, 'Bekaze I hear you say he bought yo' wil'
lan' fer a little er nothin'. He'll swindle you ef
you trade wid 'im, an' you done trade wid 'im.'
Marse Tumlin, 'low, 'Is Paul Conant ever swindle
you?' Tom Perryman say, 'No, he ain't, an' ef

he wuz ter I'd give 'im a kickin'.' Marse Tumlin
'low, ' Well, you know you is a swindler, an' nobody ain't kick you. How come dat?' Tom
Perryman say, ' Ef you say I'm a swindler, you're
a liar.'

" Well, suh, de man ain't no sooner say dat dan
bang! went Marse Tumlin's pistol, an' des ez it
banged Marse Paul Conant run 'twix' um, an' de
ball went right spang th'oo de collar-bone an' sorter
sideways th'oo de p'int er de shoulder-blade. Marse
Tumlin drapt his pistol an' cotch 'im ez he fell an'
knelt down dar by 'im, an' all de time dat ar Tom
Perryman wuz stan'in' right over um wid his pistol
in his han'. I squall out, I did, ' Whyn't some er
you white men take dat man pistol 'way fum 'im?
Don't you see what he fixin' ter do?'

" I run'd at 'im, an' he sorter flung back wid his
arm, an' when he done dat somebody grab 'im fum
behime. All dat time Marse Tumlin wuz axin'
Marse Paul Conant ef he hurt much. I hear 'im
say, ' I wouldn't 'a' done it fer de worl', Conant—
not fer de worl'.' Den de doctor, he come up, an'
Marse Tumlin, he pester de man twel he hear 'im
say, ' Don't worry, Major; dis boy'll live ter be a
older man dan you ever will.' Den Marse Tumlin
got his pistol an' hunt up an' down fer dat ar Tom

"Hunt up an' down fer dat ar Tom Perryman."

Perryman, but he done gone. I seed 'im when he got on his hoss.

"I say to Marse Tumlin, 'Ain't you des ez well ter fetch Marse Paul Conant home whar we all kin take keer uv 'im?' He 'low, 'Dat's a *fack*. Go home an' tell yo' Miss Vallie fer ter have de big room fixed up time we git dar wid 'im.' I say, 'Humph! I'll fix it myse'f; I know'd I ain't gwine ter let Miss Vallie do it.'

"Well, suh, 'tain't no use fer ter tell yer de rest. Dar's dat ar baby in dar, an' what mo' sign does you want ter show you dat it all turned out des like one er dem ol'-time tales?"

VIII

THE CASE OF MARY ELLEN

IT came to pass in due time that Atlanta, following the example of Halcyondale, organized a fair. It was called the Piedmont Exposition, and, as might be supposed, Aunt Minervy Ann was among those attracted to the city by the event. She came to see whether the fair was a bigger one than that held at Halcyondale. Naturally enough she made my house her headquarters, and her coming was fortunately timed, for the cook, taking advantage of the heavily increased demand for kitchen servants, caused by the pressure of strangers in the city, had informed us that if we wanted her services we could either double her wages or dispense with her entirely. It was a very cunningly prepared plan, for there was company in the house, friends from middle Georgia, who had come to spend a week while the exposition was going on, and there would have been no alternative if Aunt Minervy Ann, her Sunday hat sitting high on her head, had not walked in the door.

" I hope all er you-all is well," she remarked. " Ef you ain't been frettin' an' naggin' one an'er den my nose done been knocked out er j'int, kaze I know sump'n 'bleeze ter be de matter."

The truth is, the lady of the house was blazing mad with the cook, and I was somewhat put out myself, for the ultimatum of the servant meant robbery. Aunt Minervy Ann was soon in possession of the facts. At first she was properly indignant, but in a moment she began to laugh.

" Des come out on de back porch wid me, please'm. All I ax you is ter keep yo' face straight, and don't say a word less'n I ax you sump'n'." She flung her hat and satchel in a corner and sallied out. " I don't blame cooks fer wantin' ter quit when dey's so much gwine on up town," she remarked, in a loud voice, as she went out at the back door. " Dey stan' by a stove hot wedder er col', an' dey ain't got time ter go ter buryin's. But me! I don't min' de work; I'm ol' an' tough. Why, de well ain't so mighty fur fum de steps, an' dar's de wood-cellar right dar. How much you pay yo' cooks, ma'am? "

" What wages have you been getting? " asked the lady of the house.

" Wellum, down dar whar I come fum dey been payin' me four dollars a mont'—dat de reason I come up here. Ef you gi' me six I'll stay an' you won't begrudge me de money. Tu'n me loose in de kitchen an' I'm at home, ma'am—plum' at home."

The lady seemed to be hesitating, and the silence in the kitchen was oppressive.

" I'll decide to-day," she remarked. " Our cook is a good one, but she has been thinking of resting awhile. If she goes, you shall have the place."

" Den she ain't gone? " cried Aunt Minervy Ann. " Well, I don't want de place less'n she goes. I ain't gwine ter run my color out'n no job ef I kin he'p it. We got 'nuff ter contend wid des dry so." Then she turned and looked in the kitchen. " Ain't dat Julie Myrick? " she asked.

" How you know me? " cried the cook. " I b'lieve in my soul dat's Miss 'Nervy Ann Perdue! "

With that Aunt Minervy Ann went into the kitchen, and the two old acquaintances exchanged reminiscences for a quarter of an hour. After awhile she came back in the sitting-room, stared at us with a half-indignant, half-quizzical expression on her face, and then suddenly collapsed, falling on the floor near a couch, and laughing as only an old-time negro can laugh. Then she sat bolt

184

upright, and indignation, feigned or real, swept the smiles from her countenance, as if they had been suddenly wiped out with a sponge.

"You know what you got in dat kitchen dar? You ain't got nothin' in de worl' in dar but a Injun merlatter; dat zackly what you got. I know'd her daddy and I know'd her mammy. Ol' one-legged Billy Myrick wuz her daddy, an' he wuz one part white an' one part nigger, an' one part Injun. Don't tell me 'bout dem kind er tribes. Dey ain't no good in um. Hamp'll tell you dat hisse'f, an' he b'longed ter de Myrick 'state. Merlatter is bad 'nuff by itse'f, but when you put Injun wid it— well, you may hunt high an' you may hunt low, but you can't git no wuss mixtry dan dat. I tell you right now," Aunt Minervy Ann went on, "I never did see but one merlatter dat wuz wuff a pinch er snuff, an' she wuz so nigh white dat de ol' boy hisse'f couldn't 'a' tol' de diffunce. Seem like you must 'a' knowed Mary Ellen Tatum, suh?" she suggested, appealing to my memory.

I had heard the name somehow and somewhere, but it was as vague in my recollection as a dream.

"Maybe you didn't know 'er, suh, but she was born an' bred down whar I cum fum. Dat's so! She wuz done gone fum dar when you come. Wuz ol' Fed Tatum dead? Yasser! ol' Fed died de year dey quit der battlin', an' 'twuz de year atter dat when you come; an' you sho did look puny, suh, ter what you does now. Well, ol' Fed Tatum, he wuz one er deze yer quare creeturs. He made money han' over fist, an' he had a sight er niggers. He had a place sorter close ter town, but he didn't stay on it; an' he had a house not fur fum Marse Bolivar Blasengame, but he'd des go out ter his place endurin' er de day, an' den he'd come back, git his vittles, an' walk ter de tavern an' dar he'd take a cheer an' go off by hisse'f, an' set wid his chin in his coat collar, an' look at his foots an' make his thum's turn somersets over one an'er. Ef you wanted ter talk wid ol' Fed Tatum, you'd hafter go whar he wuz settin' at an' do all de talkin' yo'-se'f. He'd des set back dar an' grunt an' maybe not know who you wuz. But when he come huntin' you up, you better watch out. Dey say dey ain't nobody ever is make a trade wid ol' Fed but what dey come out at de little een' er de horn.

" Well, ol' Fed had a nigger 'oman keepin' house fer 'im, an' doin' de cookin' and washin'. I say ' nigger,' suh, but she wuz mighty nigh white. She wuz Mary Ellen's mammy, an' Mary Ellen wuz des white ez anybody, I don't keer whar dey cum

186

fum, an' she wuz purty fum de word go. Dey
wa'n't never no time, suh, atter Mary Ellen wuz
born dat she wa'n't de purtiest gal in dat town. I
des natchully 'spises merlatters, but dey wuz sump'n
'bout Mary Ellen dat allers made a lump come in
my goozle. I tuck ter dat chile, suh, de minnit I
laid my eyes on 'er. She made me think 'bout
folks I done forgot ef I ever know'd um, an' des de
sight un 'er made me think 'bout dem ol' time
chunes what mighty nigh break yo' heart when you
hear um played right. Dat wuz Mary Ellen up an'
down.

"Well, suh, when Mary Ellen got so she could
trot 'roun', old Fed Tatum sorter woke up. He
stayed at home mo', and when de sun wuz shinin'
you might see 'im any time setting in his peazzer
wid Mary Ellen playin' roun', er walkin' out in de
back yard wid Mary Ellen trottin' at his heels.
I'm telling you de start-naked trufe—by de time
dat chile wuz six-year ol' she could read; yasser!
read out'n a book, an' read good. I seed her do it
wid my own eyes, an' heer'd 'er wid my own years.
'Tain't none er dish yer readin' an' stoppin' like you
hear de school chillun gwine on; no, suh! 'Twuz
de natchual readin' right 'long. An' by de time
she wuz eight, dey wa'n't no words in no book in

dat town but what she could take an' chaw um
same as lawyers in de cote-house. Mo' dan dat,
suh, she could take a pencil, an' draw yo' likeness
right 'fo' yo' face.

" 'Long 'bout dat time she struck up wid little
Sally Blasengame, an' when dem two got tergedder
dar wuz de pick er de town ez fer ez de chillun
went. I don't say it, suh, bekaze Marse Bolivar
was Marse Tumlin's br'er-in-law—dey married
sisters—but his little gal Sally wuz ez fine ez split
silk. Mary Ellen had black hair an' big black eyes,
an' Sally had yaller hair an' big blue eyes. Atter
dey come ter know one an'er dey wa'n't a day but
what dem two chillun wuz playin' tergedder. How
many an' many is de times I seed um gwine 'long
wid der arms 'roun' one an'er!

" Well, one day atter dey been playin' tergedder
a right smart whet Marse Bolivar 'gun ter make in-
quirements 'bout Mary Ellen, an' when he foun'
out who an' what she wuz, he went out whar dey
at an' tol' her she better go home. I wuz right dar
in de back yard when he said de word. Mary Ellen
stood an' looked at 'im, an' den she picked up her
bonnet an' marched out'n de yard holdin' her head
up; she wuz twelve year ol' by den.

" Sally seed Mary Ellen go out, an' she turn
188

'roun' on her daddy, her face ez white ez a sheet. Den her whole frame 'gun ter shake. She 'low, 'I been lovin' you all dis time, an' I didn't know you could be so mean an' low-life.' She flung at 'im de fust words dat pop in her min'.

"Marse Bolivar say, 'Why, honey! Why, precious!' an' start ter put his arm 'roun' 'er. She flung fum 'im, she did, an' cry out, 'Don't you never say dem words ter me no mo' ez long ez you live, an' don't you never tetch me no mo'.' Den she seed me, an' she come runnin' des like she wuz skeer'd. She holler, 'Take me 'way! take me 'way! Don't let 'im tetch me!' Talk 'bout temper—talk 'bout venom! All dem Blasengames had it, an' when you hurt de feelin's er dat kind er folks dey are hurted sho 'nuff. Marse Bolivar couldn't 'a' looked no wuss ef somebody had 'a' spit in his face while his han's tied. You talk 'bout people lovin' der chillun, but you dunner nothin' 'tall 'bout it twel you see Marse Bolivar lovin' Sally. Why, de very groun' she walkt on wuz diffunt ter him fum any udder groun'. He wuz ready ter die fer 'er forty times a day, an' yit here she wuz wid her feelin's hurt so bad dat she won't let 'im put his han's on 'er. An' he ain't try; he had sense 'nuff fer dat. He des walk 'roun' and kick up de gravel wid de heel er his boots. But Sally, she had 'er face hid in my frock, an' she ain't so much ez look at 'im. Bimeby he went in de house, but he ain't stay dar long. He come out an' look at Sally, an' try ter make 'er talk, but she erfuse ter say a word, an' atter while he went on up-town.

" Ef dey ever wuz hard-headed folks, suh, dat wuz de tribe. He went uptown, but he ain't stay long, an' when he come back he foun' Sally in de house cryin' an' gwine on. She won't tell what de matter, an' she won't let nobody do nothin' fer 'er. Now, ef she'd 'a' been mine, suh, I'd 'a' frailed 'er out den an' dar, an' I'd 'a' kep' on frailin' 'er out twel she'd 'a' vowed dat she never know'd no gal name Mary Ellen. Dat's me! But Marse Bolivar ain't look at it dat away, an' de man what never knuckle ter no human bein', rich er po', high er low, had ter knuckle ter dat chile, an' she wa'n't much bigger dan yo' two fists.

" So bimeby he say, ' Honey, I'm gwine atter Mary Ellen, ef dat's her name, an' she can stay here all day an' all night, too, fer what I keer.'

" Sally 'low, ' She sha'n't come here! she sha'n't! I don't want nobody ter come here dat's got ter git der feelin's hurted eve'y time dey come.'

" Right dar, suh, is whar my han' would 'a' come

down hard; but Marse Bolivar, he knuckle. He
say, ' Well, honey, you'll hafter fergive me dis
time. I'll go fetch 'er ef she'll come, an' ef she
won't 'tain't my fault.'

" So out he went. I dunner how he coaxed Mary
Ellen, but she say he tol' 'er dat Sally wuz feelin'
mighty bad, an' wuz 'bleeze ter see 'er; an' Mary
Ellen, havin' mo' heart dan min', come right along.
An' Marse Bolivar wuz happy fer ter see Sally
happy.

" Dis wuz long 'fo' de battlin', suh, but even dat
fur back dey wuz talkin' 'bout war. Ol' Fed Tatum
wuz a mighty long-headed man, an' he know'd
mighty well dat ef Mary Ellen stayed dar whar she
wuz at, she won't have no mo' show dan a chicken
wid its head wrung off. So he fixed 'er up an'
packed 'er off up dar whar de Northrons is at. He'd
'a' sont her mammy wid 'er, but she say no; she'd
be in de way; folks would 'spicion what de matter
wuz; an' so she shet her mouf an' stayed. Ef Mary
Ellen had 'a' been my chile, suh, I'd 'a' gone wid
'er ef I had ter claw my way wid my naked han's
thoo forty miles er brick wall. But her mammy
was diffunt; she stayed an' pined.

" Now, ef anybody want pinin' done dey'll hafter
go ter somebody else 'sides ol' Minervy Ann Per-

due. When you see me pinin', suh, you may know my tongue done cut out an' my han's pairlized. Ef Mary Ellen had 'a' been my chile dey'd 'a' been murder done, suh. I'd 'a' cotch ol' Fed Tatum by what little hair he had an' I'd 'a' ruint 'im; an' ez 'twuz, I come mighty nigh havin' a fight wid 'im. An' ef I had—*ef I had*——"

Aunt Minervy Ann was on her feet. Her right arm was raised high in the air, and her eyes blazed with passion. It was not a glimpse of temper she gave us, but a fleeting portrayal of mother-love at white heat. She had been carried away by her memory, and had carried us away with her; but she caught herself, as it were, in the act, laughed, and sat down again by the sofa, caressing it with both arms. Presently she resumed her narrative, addressing herself this time to the lady of the house. It was a stroke of rare tact that had its effect.

" Wellum, Mary Ellen wa'n't my chile, an' ol' Fed Tatum sont 'er off up dar 'mongst de Northrons; an' 'bout de time de two sides 'gun der battlin' he sol' some lan' an' sont her 'nuff money ter las' 'er twel she got all de larnin' she want. Den de war come, an' nobody ain't hear no mo' 'bout Mary Ellen. Dey fit an' dey fout, an' dey fout an' dey fit, an' den, bimeby, dey quit, an' fer long

192

days nobody didn't know whedder ter walk back-
erds er go forruds.

" Ol' Fed Tatum wuz one er dem kinder folks,
ma'am, what you been seein' an' knowin' so long
dat you kinder git de idee dey er gwine ter stay des
like dey is; but one day ol' Fed Tatum fetch'd a
grunt an' went ter bed, an' de nex' day he fetch'd
a groan an' died. He sho did. An' den when dey
come ter look into what he had, dey foun' dat he
ain't got nothin' he kin call his own but a little cabin
in one een' er town, an' dis went ter Mary Ellen's
mammy.

" I tell you now, ma'am, dat 'oman tried me.
She wuz long an' lank an' slabsided, an' she went
'bout wid 'er mouf shet, an' 'er cloze lookin' like
somebody had flung um at 'er. I like ter hear folks
talk, myself, an' ef dey can't do nothin' else I like
ter see um show dey temper. But dat 'oman, she
des walk 'roun' an' not open her mouf fum mornin'
twel night, less'n you ax 'er sump'n. I tried ter git
her ter talk 'bout Mary Ellen, but she ain't know
no mo' 'bout Mary Ellen dan a rabbit.

" I dunner but what we'd 'a' got in a fuss, ma'am,
kaze dat 'oman sho did try me, but 'long 'bout dat
time Marse Bolivar's gal tuck sick, an' 'twa'n't long
'fo' she died. 'Twuz a mighty pity, too, kaze dat

chile would 'a' made a fine 'oman—none better.
'Long todes de las' she got ter gwine on 'bout Mary
Ellen. Look like she could see Mary Ellen in de
fever-dreams, an' she'd laugh an' go on des like
she useter when she wuz a little bit er gal.

"Wellum, when dat chile died Marse Bolivar
come mighty nigh losin' 'is min'. He ain't make
no fuss 'bout it, but he des fell back on hisse'f an'
walk de flo' night atter night, an' moan an' groan
when he think nobody ain't lis'nin'. An' den, atter
so long a time, here come a letter fum Mary Ellen,
an' dat broke 'im all up. I tell you right now,
ma'am, Marse Bolivar had a hard fight wid trouble.
I don't keer what folks may say; dey may tell you
he's a hard man, ready ter fight an' quick ter kill.
He's all dat, an' maybe mo'; but I know what I
know.

"Wellum, de days went an' de days come.
Bimeby I hear some er de niggers say dat Mary
Ellen done come back. I laid off ter go an' see de
chile; but one day I wuz gwine 'long de street an' I
met a white lady. She say, ' Ain't dat Aunt Minervy Ann?' I 'low, ' Yessum, dis is de remnants.'
Wid dat, ma'am, she grab me 'roun' de neck an'
hug me, an' bu'st out a-cryin', an' 'twa'n't nobody
in de worl' but Mary Ellen.

" Purty! I never has foun' out, ma'am, how any human can be ez purty ez Mary Ellen. Her skin wuz white ez milk an' her eyes shine like stars. I'd 'a' never know'd her in de worl'. But dar she wuz, cryin' one minnit an' laughin' de nex'. An' she wuz in trouble too. She had a telegraph in her han' tellin' 'er dat one er her ol' schoolmates gwine on ter Flurridy wuz gwine ter stop over one train des ter see Mary Ellen. Hit seem like dat up dar whar she been stayin' at she ain't never tell nobody but what she wuz white, an' de human wa'n't born dat could tell de diffunce. So dar 'twuz. Here wuz de Northron lady comin' fer ter see Mary Ellen, an' what wuz Mary Ellen gwine ter do?—whar wuz she gwine ter take de Northron lady? Dar wuz de ramshackle cabin, an' dar wuz my kitchen. You may think 'twuz funny, ma'am——"

" But I don't," said the lady of the house, abruptly and unexpectedly; " I don't think it was funny at all."

Aunt Minervy Ann looked at me and lifted her chin triumphantly, as she resumed: "No'm, 'twa'n't funny. Mary Ellen wuz proud an' high-strung; you could read dat in de way she walk an' eve'y motion she make, an' dat ar telegraph dat de Northron lady sont 'er fum Atlanty kinder run 'er in a corner. She dunner what ter do, ner which way ter turn. Look at it yo'se'f, ma'am, an' see whar she wuz.

"She laughed, ma'am, but she wuz in trouble, an' I'm sech a big fool dat I'm allers in trouble 'long wid dem what I like. Take de tape-line ter der trouble an' den ter mine, an' you'll fin' dat dey medjer 'bout de same. Mary Ellen laugh an' say, 'Dey's two things I kin do; I kin leave town, er I kin go down dar ter de cabin an' kill myse'f.' Oh, she wuz in a corner, ma'am—don't you doubt it.

"Right den an' dar sump'n pop in my head. I 'low, 'Is you been ter call on Marse Bolivar Blasengame?' She say 'No, I ain't, Aunt Minervy Ann. I started ter go, but I'm afear'd ter.' I 'low, 'Well, I'm gwine dar right now; come go wid me.'

"So we went dar, and I left Mary Ellen on de back porch, an' I went in de house. Marse Bolivar wuz settin' down, gwine over some papers, an' Mis' Em'ly wuz darnin' an' patchin'.

"I say, 'Marse Bolivar, dey's a gal out here dat I thought maybe you an' Mis' Em'ly would be glad ter see?'"

"He 'low, 'Dang you' hide, Minervy Ann! You

like ter make me jump out'n my skin. Who is de
gal?'

"I say, 'I wanter see ef you know 'er.' Wid
dat I went back an' fotch Mary Ellen in. Well, dey
didn't know 'er, ma'am, na'er one un um; an' I
dunner how it all happened, but de fust thing I
know Mary Ellen fell on 'er knees, by a lounge what
sot under de place whar Miss Sally's pictur' wuz
hangin' at. She fell on her knees, Mary Ellen did,
and 'low, 'She'd know who I is,' an' wid dat she
bust aloose an' went ter cryin' des like 'er heart wuz
done broke in two.

"Marse Bolivar stood dar an' wait twel Mary
Ellen cool off, an' quiet down. Mis' Em'ly, ma'am,
is one er dem ar primity, dried-up wimmen, which,
ef dey ain't fightin' you wid bofe han's, er huggin'
you wid bofe arms, ain't sayin' nothin' 'tall. An'
ef Mis' Em'ly ain't sayin' nothin' you can't put de
key in de Bible an' fin' no tex' dat'll tell you what
she got in 'er min'. But she wuz darnin', an' I see
'er wipe one eye on de leg er de sock, an' den present'y she wipe t'er eye.

"Wellum, Marse Bolivar stood dar an' look at
Mary Ellen, an' when she riz fum her knees an'
stood dar, her head hangin' down, still a-cryin', but
mo' quieter, he went close up an' 'low, 'I know you,
197

Mary Ellen, an' I'm mighty glad ter see you. Dat ar letter what you writ me, I got it yit, an' I'm gwine ter keep it whiles I live.'

" He talk right husky, ma'am, an' I 'gun ter feel husky myse'f; an' den I know'd dat ef I didn't change de tune, I'd be boo-hooin' right dar 'fo' all un um wid needer 'casion nor 'skuce. I went up ter Mary Ellen an' cotch 'er by de shoulder and say, ' Shucks, gal! Dat train'll be here terreckly, an' den what you gwine ter do? '

" 'Twuz a hint ez broad ez a horse-blanket, ma'am, but Mary Ellen never tuck it. She des stood dar an' look at me. An' 'bout dat time Marse Bolivar he ketch'd holt er my shoulder an' whirlt me 'roun', an' 'low, ' What de matter, Minervy Ann? Talk it right out! '

" Wellum, I let you know I tol' 'im; I des laid it off! I tol' des how 'twuz; how Mary Ellen been sont up dar by ol' Fed Tatum, an' how, on de 'count er no fault er her'n de Northron folks tuck 'er ter be a white gal; an' how one er de gals what went ter school wid 'er wuz gwine ter come ter see 'er an' stay 'twixt trains. Den I 'low, ' Whar is Mary Ellen gwine ter see 'er? In dat ar mud-shack whar her ma live at? In de big road? In de woods? In de hoss-lot? ' "

The whole scene from beginning to end had been enacted by Aunt Minervy Ann. In the empty spaces of the room she had placed the colonel, his wife, and Mary Ellen, and they seemed to be before us, and not only before us, but the passionate earnestness with which she laid the case of Mary Ellen before the colonel made them live and move under our very eyes.

"*In de big road? In de woods? In de hoss-lot?*"

And when she paused for the reply of the colonel, the look of expectation on her face was as keen and as eager as it could have been on the day and the occasion when she was pleading for Mary Ellen. The spell was broken by the lady of the house, who leaned forward eagerly as if expecting the colonel himself to reply. Perhaps Aunt Minervy Ann misunderstood the movement. She paused a moment as if dazed, and then sank by the sofa with a foolish laugh.

"I know you all put me down ter be a fool," she said, "an' I 'speck I is."

"Nonsense!" cried the lady of the house, sharply. "What did the colonel reply?"

Aunt Minervy remained silent a little while, picking at one of the fringes of the sofa. She was

199

evidently trying to reassemble in her mind the incidents and surroundings of her narrative. Presently she began again, in a tone subdued and confidential:

"Marse Bolivar look at me right hard, den he look at Mary Ellen, an' den he pull at de tip-een' er his year. Wellum, I fair helt my breff; I say ter myse'f, 'Man, whyn't you look at poor Miss Sally's pictur'? I wuz feared a fly might light on 'im an' change his min'. But, look at de pictur' he did, an' dat settled it.

"He 'low, 'Set down, Mary Ellen; you look tired. Minervy Ann, fetch 'er a drink er water.' Wellum, you may well b'lieve dat I flied up an' flew'd 'roun' an' fotch dat water. Den he 'low, 'Minervy Ann, go in dar an' straighten out dat parlor; fling open de blinds an' do 'bout in dar!'"

Again Aunt Minervy Ann arose from her reclining position by the sofa and stood in the floor; again, by a wave of her hand, she brought the scene before our eyes.

"I stood dar, I did, an' look at dat man. I 'low, 'Marse Bolivar, less'n it's Marse Tumlin, youer de bes' man dat God A'mighty ever breathe de breath er life inter!' He rub his han' over his face an'

say, ' Dang yo' ol' hide! go on an' hush up! Fum
de time I fust know'd you, you been gittin' me an'
Tumlin in hot water.'

" I flung back at 'im, *''Tain't never scald you!
'Tain't never been too deep fer you!'* He straight-
en hisse'f up an' helt his head back an' laugh. He
'low, ' Dang it all, Minervy Ann! Dey er times
when I want it bofe hot an' deep. You go an'
scuffle 'roun' in dat parlor, an' don't you let yo' Mis'
Em'ly do a han's-turn in dar.'

" Wellum, dat uz 'bout de upshot un it. De
Northron lady wuz name Miss Wilbur, er Willard,
I disremember which, but she was a mighty nice
white gal. Marse Bolivar an' Hamp wuz bofe at de
train ter meet 'er, an' Marse Bolivar fotch 'er right
ter de house, an' show'd 'er in de parlor. Atter
while, Mary Ellen went in dar, an' 'twuz a mighty
meetin' 'twix um. Dey chattered same ez a flock
er blackbirds on a windy day; an' atter so long a
time Marse Bolivar went in dar. 'Twa'n't long 'fo'
he got ter tellin' tales, an' de Northron lady laugh
so she kin hardly set on de cheer. Den he open de
pianner, an' ax de white lady ter play, but she vow
she can't play atter he been hearin' Mary Ellen.
Den he say, ' Won't you play me a chune, Mary
Ellen? Sump'n ol' timey?'

" Dat gal went ter de pianner, ma'am, an' sot dar wid her han's over her face like she prayin', an' den she laid her han's on de keys an' started a chune des like yo' hear in yo' dreams. It got a little louder, an' den present'y you could hear 'er singin'. I never did know whar'bouts her voice slipped inter dat chune; but dar 'twuz, an' it fit in wid de pianner des like a flute does.

" Wellum, it tuck me back, way back dar in de ol' days, an' den brung me down ter later times, fer many a moonlight night did I hear Miss Sally an' Mary Ellen sing dat song when dey wuz chillun. Den atter dat de Northron lady plump herse'f down at de pianner, an' she sho did shake dat ol' shebang up. 'Twuz dish yer highfalutin' music what sprung up sence de war, an' it sho sound like war ter me, drums a-rattlin', guns a-shootin', an' forty-levm brass horns all tootin' a diffunt chune.

" When train-time come, ma'am, de Northron lady ax Mary Ellen ef she won't go ter de train wid 'er. But Marse Bolivar spoke up an' say dat Mary Ellen been feelin' bad all de mornin', an' she hatter skuzen 'er. He went wid de lady hisse'f, an' when he come back Mary Ellen tol' 'im she never would fergit what he done fer her dat day, an' say she gwine ter pay 'im back some day.

" What did the neighbors say about it? " the lady of the house asked, in her practical way.

" Dat what pestered me all de time, ma'am," Aunt Minervy Ann replied. " I ax Marse Bolivar, ' What de folks gwine ter say when dey hear 'bout dis come off? ' He stuck his thum's in de arm-holes er his wescut, an' 'low, ' Dat what I wanter know, an' I wanter know so bad, Minervy Ann, dat ef you hear anybody talkin' loose talk 'bout it, des come runnin' ter me while it's hot. Now don't you fail.'

" But Marse Bolivar ain't wait fer me ter hear what folks say. He went polin' up town de nex' day, an' tol' 'bout it in eve'y sto' on de street, an' de las' man in town vow'd 'twuz de ve'y thing ter do. An' dat ain't all, ma'am! De folks dar raise a lot er money fer Mary Ellen, an' de way dat chile went on when Marse Bolivar put it in 'er han' an' tol' er whar it come fum wuz pitiful ter see.

" Dat's de way 'tis, ma'am; ketch um in de hu-mor an' eve'ybody's good; ketch um out'n de hu-mor an' dey er all mean—I know dat by my own feelin's. Ef a fly had lit on Marse Bolivar's face dat day, Mary Ellen would 'a' had ter face 'er trouble by 'er own 'lone self. Ef some sour-minded man had gone up town an' told how Marse Bolivar wuz en'tainin' nigger gals an' a Yankee 'oman in his parlor, dey'd all been down on 'im. An' den——"

" What, then? " the lady of the house asked, as Aunt Minervy Ann paused.

" Dey'd 'a' been weepin' an' whailin' in de settlement sho. Ain't it so, suh? "

It was natural, after Aunt Minervy Ann had narrated the particulars of this episode, that her statements should dwell in my memory, and sally forth and engage my mind when it should have been concerned with other duties. One of these duties was to examine each day the principal newspapers of New England in search of topics for editorial comment.

An eye trained to this business, as any exchange editor can tell you, will pick out at a glance a familiar name or suggestive phrase, no matter what its surroundings nor how obscurely it may be printed. Therefore, one day, weeks after Aunt Minervy Ann's recital, when I opened the *Boston Transcript* at its editorial page, it was inevitable that the first thing to catch my eye was the familiar name of " Mary Ellen Tatum." It was printed in type of the kind called nonpareil, but I would have seen it no sooner nor more certainly if it had been printed in letters reaching half across the page.

Mary Ellen Tatum! The name occurred in a three-line preface to the translation of an art note from a Paris newspaper. This note described, with genuine French enthusiasm, the deep impression that had been made on artists and art circles in Paris by a portrait painted by a gifted young American artist, Mlle. Marie Helen Tatum. It is needless to transcribe the eulogy—I have it in my scrap-book. It was a glowing tribute to a piece of work that had created a sensation, and closed with the announcement that another genius had " arrived."

The comments of the Boston editor, following the sketch, declared that the friends of Miss Mary Ellen Tatum in Boston, where she spent her early years and where she was educated, were proud of her remarkable success, and predicted for her a glorious career as an artist.

I had no more than cut this piece from the newspaper when the door-bell rang, and as there happened to be no one in the house to answer it at the moment, I went to the door myself, the clipping still in my hand, and there before my eyes was Colonel Bolivar Blasengame, his fine face beaming with good-nature. He had come at a moment when I most desired to see him, and I greeted him cordially.

"I see now," said the colonel, "why it is I can never catch you in your office in town; you do your work at home. Well, that's lots better than workin' where any and everybody can come in on you. I thought I'd find you out here enjoying your *otium cum digitalis,* as old Tuck Bonner used to say; but instead of that you're waist-deep in newspapers."

I assured the colonel that there were some people in the world whom I would be glad to see, no matter how busy I might be.

"I know the feeling," replied Colonel Blasengame; "but you'll be cussing me as sure as the world, for I haven't a grain of business to see you about. But I hear Tumlin and old Aunt Minervy Ann talking about you so constantly that I thought I'd come out and say howdye, if no more."

"Well, you'll have to say more than that this time," I remarked; "I was just thinking, when you rang the door-bell, that I would give something pretty to see you."

"Now, is that reely so?" cried the colonel. "Then I'm twice glad—once because I took a no-

tion to come, and once again because you're glad.
You used to fight so shy of me when you lived
among us that I was afraid I wouldn't get on wi'
you; but I'm sorter offish myself."

"Colonel," said I, "did you ever know Mary
Ellen Tatum?"

He rubbed his face and forehead with his hand,
and regarded me with a slight frown, and a smile
that seemed to mean anything except pleasure.

"Will you allow me to ask you why you put
such a question to me?"

"Why, certainly, Colonel; read that." I placed
the clipping from the *Transcript* in his hand. He
held it off at arm's length and tried to decipher it,
but the print was too fine. Placing it on his knee,
he searched in his pockets until he found his specta-
cles, and then he read the article through carefully
—not once, but twice.

Then smoothing the clipping out on his knee, he
looked at me inquiringly.

"Do you know Mary Ellen?" he asked. I did
not, and said so. "Did you ever hear of her before?"

"Why, yes," I replied. "Aunt Minervy Ann
told me some very interesting things about her, and
I wanted to ask you if they were true."

The colonel jumped to his feet with a laugh. "Plague on old Minervy Ann!" he exclaimed. "Why, I came out here purposely to tell you about Mary Ellen. This thing," indicating the clipping, "is away behind the time with its news. The picture it tells about is at my house this very minute, and another one in the bargain. The first chance you get, come down home and look at 'em. If you don't open your eyes I'll never sign my name S. B. Blasengame again." He walked up and down the room in a restless way. "What do you reckon that gyurl did?" he asked, stopping before me and stretching out his right arm. "Why, she sent a man with the pictures—a right nice fellow he was, too. He said it cost a pile of money to git 'em through the custom-house at New York; he had to hang around there a week. When I asked him for his bill he raised his hands and laughed. Everything was paid."

The colonel continued to walk up and down the room. He was always restless when anything interested him, unless it happened to be a matter of life and death, and then he was calmness itself.

"Did Aunt Minervy Ann—blame her old hide! —I wanted to tell you the whole story myself—did

she tell you about a letter Mary Ellen wrote me
when "—the colonel paused and cleared his throat
—" about a letter Mary Ellen wrote me in the
seventies?"

" She did," I replied.

" Well, here's the letter," he said, after fum-
bling in his big pocketbook. " It's not a matter to
be showing around, but you seem almost like one
of the family, and you'll know better how to appre-
ciate the pictures when you read that."

He turned and went out of the room into the
hallway and then to the veranda, where I heard his
firm and measured step pacing back and forth. The
letter was not a very long one, but there was something in it—a vague undertone of loneliness, a
muffled cry for sympathy, which, as I knew all the
facts of the case, almost took my breath away.

The letter was dated " Boston, September 8th,
1878," and was as follows:

" COLONEL BLASENGAME—Two days ago the home
paper came to me bringing the news of the great loss
which has come to your household, and to me. I feel
most keenly that a letter from me is an unwarranted
intrusion, but I must speak out my thoughts to someone. Miss Sallie was almost the only friend I had when
she and I were children together—almost the only per-
son that I ever cared for. I loved her while she lived,
and I shall cherish her memory to the day of my death.

" You do not know me, and you will not recognize the name signed to this. It is better, far better that this should be so. It is enough for you to know that a stranger in a strange land will lie awake many and many a long night, weeping for the dear young lady who is dead.

" MARY ELLEN TATUM."

What has become of Mary Ellen? the reader may ask. I have asked the same question hundreds of times and received no reply to it. So far as we provincials are concerned, she has disappeared utterly from the face of the earth.